THOMAS McNULTY

COFFIN FOR AN OUTLAW

Complete and Unabridged

LINFORD
Leicester

First published in Great Britain in 2015 by
Robert Hale Limited
London

First Linford Edition
published 2018
by arrangement with
Robert Hale
an imprint of The Crowood Press
Wiltshire

A catalogue record for this book is available
from the British Library.

ISBN 978–1–4448–3695–0

Published by
F. A. Thorpe (Publishing)
Anstey, Leicestershire

Set by Words & Graphics Ltd.
Anstey, Leicestershire
Printed and bound in Great Britain by
T. J. International Ltd., Padstow, Cornwall

This book is printed on acid-free paper

*Dedicated to my lovely wife Jan
And our gunslinging friends
Brent Boyd and Corena Boyd
Saddle Up!*

1

When the rolling grasslands gave way he spent five days amongst the chiseled spires and ragged ridges of the badlands. He traveled south on a buckboard. The land was dry, forlorn, bleached with heat and loneliness and an unrelenting despair. The centuries of wind and rain and sun had turned the gullies and valleys into a no-man's-land. The cliffs seemed like brown beasts lurking at every turn, sentinels of the unknown measuring his journey with an impartial stare.

On the second day the Cheyenne came to observe him. They sat astride their ponies watching with stoic expressions. Word had come down from the Cheyenne camps, telling of the white man taking a coffin on his journey of death. The coffin was in the buckboard, cut from pine with his own blistered hands, nailed together, and resting under a tarpaulin. He ignored the Cheyenne because they offered no threat. His was a journey all men make, but not all men carry a coffin with them.

The badlands would be the more physically demanding part of his journey. It was the heat that was dangerous. He had prepared carefully and brought an ample supply of water. He could have planned a longer route and circled the badlands before striking into Nebraska, but he knew the story would spread. That was important. The shortest route was through the badlands.

He was almost out of the badlands when he picked up his first rider. *No hurry*, he thought, *they know who I am now so it doesn't matter*. He shook the reins and made a clicking sound with his tongue. The horse pulling his buckboard perked its ears and started walking again. He had stopped for ten minutes to drink some water from his canteen and to give the horse water, too. But then he'd seen the dust in the air. Maybe three miles ahead. So they were on to him.

He wasn't the type of man to worry. Some gunmen, at first hint of conflict, would instinctively pull out their Peacemaker and check the cylinder. Some even went so far as to load a sixth cartridge in the empty chamber, but he thought that was plain foolishness. He'd seen too many Peacemakers discharge accidentally because some damn fool had loaded six. That firing pin on the hammer could easily be jostled. Once, when he was still young and new to gunfighting, he'd almost blown his foot off when he went to draw his gun. His thumb had brushed the hammer and the detonation had sent that bullet slamming down the side of his leg. His leg carried a long, snaking scar as a reminder. No, five would do it. A gunfighter who couldn't finish a man with five shouldn't be packing a gun.

There were two riders. He could see

them clearly now. They had come in from the south. He thought the telegraph would have hummed the news, far north of his current position. It would have sung along the wires and made its way to Nebraska. The story had reached his enemies and now they would test him.

He went another mile before stopping. The two riders split apart, coming at him on each side. He took off his hat, unstrung his bandanna from about his neck and wiped the perspiration from his brow. Then he wiped out his Stetson before returning it to his head. They were smart to come at him on each side. They would believe they held the advantage, thinking that no man could defend himself from the left and right simultaneously. It would have worked against the average man.

They rode up cautiously, two men in their early thirties, gunfighters by the look of them.

'Howdy mister,' the man on the left said.

He remained silent, scrutinizing them.

'My friend said howdy,' the man on the right said.

Still he remained silent, but all the while he was calculating, assessing each man's strengths and weaknesses. He finally determined the man on the right would draw first.

'You gonna say something?' the man on the right said. 'We don't take lightly to being treated rudely.'

'We're just being friendly is all,' the man on the left said. 'Seeing how you're all alone out here we wanted to be neighborly.'

He allowed himself a long pause before saying, 'Let's get to the dance. I don't have all day.'

The two men looked at each other.

'You're him, then? You're Chance Sonnet?' The man on the left had spoken.

'I'm him.'

'They said you died fifteen years ago in Missouri.'

Again he reverted to a silent stare.

'You carrying a coffin to Eric Cabot?'

'I am,' he replied.

'Let's see it,' the man on the left said. 'But keep your hand away from your gun.'

Sonnet frowned, turned in his seat and with his left hand flipped the tarpaulin off the coffin.

'I'll be damned!' said the man on the left.

'Yes, you are,' Sonnet told him.

The man raised an eyebrow. 'What was that you said?'

Sonnet looked him in the eye but his attention was in his peripheral vision. As he stared at the man on the left, who suddenly seemed to realize he was doomed along with his partner, the other man drew his gun. Sonnet's gun streaked upward and the muzzle roared, spitting flame and lead. The man took the bullet in his chest and toppled. The man on the left had pulled his gun but his horse bucked, as Sonnet knew it would, and before the man could pull back the hammer Sonnet's gun roared again. The man twisted from his saddle, a blossom of red bursting across his ribs. He fell to the ground in a cloud of dust.

Sonnet grabbed the reins and said to his horse, 'Easy, boy.' The horse, which had been startled by the gunfire, held its ground. He waited for the dust to settle.

The two riderless horses had cantered off but now stood together on a knoll. Sonnet went to the horses first and pulled a Winchester from each saddle boot. Then he removed the saddles and swatted each animal on the rump. They scampered away as he searched the saddlebags. He came up with some dried beef and biscuits and added that to his food supply. Then he climbed on the buckboard and lifted the coffin lid. He set the two Winchesters inside the coffin.

Finally Sonnet turned his attention to the dead men. He stripped off their gunbelts and added the holsters and guns to the coffin. Then he searched their pockets. He went about his task methodically, without remorse, ignoring the ghastly stares of their unseeing eyes. He wasn't squeamish, but he didn't linger any longer than he had to.

He placed the lid on to the coffin and covered it again with the tarp. Then he fetched the saddles and set them on the buckboard. They would add some weight and slow him down but he could sell them in the next town. Then he returned to the bodies. He crossed their arms over their chests and lined them up in the dust side by side.

'Very neat and orderly,' he said aloud. His horse pricked its ears.

And so the gunman Chance Sonnet, long rumored to be dead, scout for Custer, former Texas Ranger, Indian fighter and protector of whores, sat himself on his buckboard to continue his journey into Nebraska on his way to Dodge City, Kansas. It was the 15th of May, 1887. Sonnet reckoned if his luck didn't hold he'd be dead in under two weeks. But why worry about it now? Today had been a good one and it wasn't even high noon. He was pleased by the day's bounty. He'd acquired two Winchesters, two Colt revolvers with holsters, ammunition, biscuits, two saddles for the selling, and two twenty-dollar gold pieces! That amounted to a small fortune.

He picked up the reins and made a clicking sound with his tongue. His obedient horse began walking. Sonnet hoped they could travel fifteen more miles before sunset.

2

Fear is not something that men often speak about. Fear is something they prefer to keep close to their vests, like cards in a poker game. To reveal their fear is, for some men, a sign of weakness. Chance Sonnet knew fear and accepted it. From his way of thinking to acknowledge that he was afraid was a sign of inner strength. He would not be beaten. And, if necessary, he would die with his boots on, like his friend Custer had long ago on a dusty Montana hilltop.

Once on to the plains of Nebraska he made camp near a cluster of trees. He made a small fire and drank a tin cup of hot coffee. The sun melted into the dust and the darkness wrapped its impenetrable blanket around his camp. Darkness so thick that he felt he might suffocate. He added a few twigs to the fire. He was mesmerized by the flames. He watched the fire until all that remained was a golden husk of glowing coals. He added more kindling and a few short logs that he scrounged out of the deadfall around the trees. The fire blazed to life.

There was nothing to do, nobody to talk with.

The darkness crept closer. Presently he heard small animals foraging in a thicket. Somewhere in the distance a coyote howled. Some time later an owl hooted and he thought perhaps it was really a Cheyenne Indian. No matter, they would leave him to his ghosts.

His eyelids began to droop and he accepted that sleep was coming. Each night it was the same. He attempted to stave off sleep but eventually his tired body and mind succumbed and he slept.

He didn't enjoy sleeping because that was when the dreams began.

* * *

It wasn't long before she entered the clearing and stood next to his campfire. She never spoke but she smiled. Lauren had a beautiful smile. But Chance couldn't look at her for too long because of the rope burn on her neck. She wore a simple cotton dress and walked barefoot through the warm summer grass. He recalled the way her chestnut hair sometimes caught the light, and when she turned and smiled at him something broke open deep inside and everything that he had lost in life was alive again. Her teeth were pearl-white, her skin bronze from the sun, her eyes the blue of an ocean.

Then a dark wind blew across the Nebraska prairie and snuffed out his fire. The embers glowed eerily in the midnight blackness. He smelled the pungent earth, the smoke from his fire, his sweat drying on his body. Then he smelled death and heard the creak of timbers from the weight of her body swinging on the rope. He cried out and briefly awoke. A light breeze brushed through the trees, making a sound like soft wings beating gently.

The stars twinkled in the velvet sky like razor tips. He watched them in wonderment. How vast was the universe, he wondered? How long had men crawled upon the earth before standing upright and learning how to kill? He thought that all of human history was ripe with murder. He no longer found solace in the earth's beauty. What peace of mind he'd known lasted but a few short years when he took the name of Frank Neal and set aside his gun to become a carpenter.

Finally, he slept.

★   ★   ★

He awoke at dawn to a black sky. The storm had slipped in from the northwest and positioned itself over the prairie like a slumbering leviathan. A mass of lavender clouds boiled with fury, lightning crackling along the purple ridges. His horse began to stomp restlessly. He uncoiled the reins and let the horse fend for itself. It would be easier on the animal than letting it thrash in blind panic when the storm hit. He examined his position, satisfied that he was safe from a downpour. The danger was being caught in a gully, which would fill quickly with rainwater. Many a pilgrim had learned the hard lessons the frontier offered and paid for their ignorance with their lives. Drowning in a flash flood was a danger too many had ignored. The water's strength was easily underestimated and it could sweep through a ravine with the power of a locomotive.

Thunder boomed in the distance and the air turned cold. He would have preferred a better location but this small section of hills bordered by a thin group of pines would suffice. He found his duster, pulled it on and waited. Within thirty minutes he could smell the rain and the electricity crackled madly in the heavens. Sonnet crawled under the wagon.

The storm began with a few isolated raindrops splattering the wagon, then it came down in raging torrents. The wind ranted and screeched like a banshee. The world turned into a raging battle of wind and rain and thunder and lightning. The wagon shook from the storm's ferocity. He was relatively safe from the rain, although the ground around him soaked up the water quickly. Before long he was lying flat on the only dry patch of earth in northern Nebraska. The coffin and tarpaulin above him prevented most of the leakage that would have normally soaked him.

He wasn't tired but he drifted into another restless slumber. Lauren's body swung back and forth on a rope and her ghost screamed at him from the black sky. When he awoke the wind had abated somewhat but the rain still pattered against the wagon. He realized that at that moment he was as safe as anyone could hope to be, no matter that a fierce thunderstorm raged above him. Hunkered down under the wagon, he was far removed from the series of events set in motion all those long months ago when Lauren was still alive.

Now Eric Cabot would be waiting on him. An image of Cabot's features floated to the surface of his memory. Tall, heavyset with eyes like the brown markings on a fat potato. His thin, cruel lips were an anomaly on his beefy features. Sonnet estimated that Cabot had three inches in height on him and at least a hundred pounds. The man gave the appearance of strength. Sonnet felt instinctively that he could best him in a fistfight. His objective was to see Cabot beaten, crushed and with nowhere to run.

An hour later the rain had stopped and Sonnet pulled himself from under the wagon. It took another hour before he found his horse, two miles away and nibbling at the wet grass near a circle of trees. The morning was gone and he wouldn't make much progress, but there wasn't any hurry. *No*, he thought to himself, *there's no hurry at all*. Killing was something a man should take his time with.

The following day he pulled into a town without a name. It was more of a ramshackle settlement that might become a town, although it was unlikely. It was too far from the railroad and the river. He thought it was more of a stopping-off place for a group of pilgrims that had simply run out of energy and enthusiasm. There were a lot of forlorn settlements like this in the West: six or seven buildings set along an old wagon trail. A nothing little place where the inhabitants were pale-skinned with tired expressions that reminded him of old dogs that had trouble mustering the energy to chase cats. Old dogs that had seen their day and lounged about while the flies buzzed around them.

There was a man sitting on a creaky boardwalk in front of a saloon. Sonnet pulled the buckboard's wheel brace into place and studied the man. He was

17

maybe thirty, older in spirit.

'I have goods to sell,' Sonnet announced. 'Who might I see in this town?'

'Nobody here has much money.'

'I have two saddles. I can sell them at a lower price than you'll find anywhere, or I can trade.'

'I was speaking English, mister.'

Sonnet climbed off the wagon. The man was smoking a thin cigar. It gave off a foul smell. Sonnet looked the man in the eye. 'That cigar smells as bad as you,' he remarked. Then he brushed past the man and entered the saloon.

The place was pieced together with planks and wood barrels. Whatever liquor they served was probably distilled in the back room. A fat, red-headed woman wearing bloomers sat at a table, sipping from a glass. She was short, and her stumpy legs reminded Sonnet of a pig's legs, pale and plump. He thought she was too damned ugly to be a whore. She flashed a toothless smile.

The barkeep was tall and young. He looked cleaner than the fat woman but only a tad friendlier than the man out on the boardwalk. He had a slender face and a receding hairline. He eyed Sonnet suspiciously.

'How can I help you?'

'I have two saddles to sell or trade. Name your price.'

'I can't afford any saddles. This isn't exactly the Metropolitan in Chicago.'

'There a restaurant in town?'

'Nope, but Sandra here can cook up some eggs. Got some bread, too.'

Sandra pushed herself up from her chair. The rolls of fat around her midsection jiggled beneath the thin fabric of her blouse. Sonnet felt a chill run down his spine. She was just one damn unsightly woman.

'Are the eggs fresh?'

'We got chickens out back. Look for yourself, mister.'

Sonnet went out the back and surveyed the alley. There was a chicken coop and further down a pen with three horses. The horses looked old. Sonnet went back and ordered the eggs and bread. He sat at a table and smoked while Sandra went to work getting his food ready. He had to eat and the eggs would help.

The man from the boardwalk came in and sat at Sonnet's table.

'You gonna eat?' the man asked.

'Not that it's any of your business, but I am.'

'I looked at those saddles on your wagon. That's some nice leather. The one has silver conchos. Nobody around here can afford to buy saddles like that. How did you come by them?'

'I shot the two men that owned them, set the horses free and kept the saddles. I'll give you a nice price.'

The room was silent. Sonnet felt the barkeep's eyes on him. The man across from him blanched.

'You say you shot the men?'

Sonnet frowned. 'I was speaking English, mister.'

The man's eyes went wide and his

face turned red.

'Here now . . . I mean . . . I didn't mean nothin' outside. We don't get many travelers. This ain't much of a crossroads.'

The man looked away, embarrassed.

'All right,' Sonnet said, 'There's got to be somebody in this town with money. It doesn't have to be much. I need to lighten the load on that wagon.'

'Mister, I've got five dollars to my name.'

'Same here,' the barkeep said behind them.

'Fine.' Sonnet dropped his cheroot on the floor and ground it with his boot heel. 'Five dollars a saddle.'

The man's jaw dropped in astonishment. The barkeep said, 'Say that again.'

'Five dollars a saddle.'

'Why, you're plumb loco, mister! Those saddles are worth a sight more than that!'

'I don't have time to look for a buyer. You want the saddles or not? One for each of you.'

21

The two men looked at each other.

The barkeep said, 'This ain't no trick?'

'Nope.'

'Well, mister if you're crazy enough to sell those saddles for five dollars apiece I reckon I'll take one.'

'And I'll take the other,' the barkeep said.

They came up with the coins quick enough and Sonnet instructed both men to clear the saddles off his wagon and to load the wagon with the supplies that he wrote down on a piece of paper: bacon, flour, sugar, coffee. They went out together as Sandra brought his plate of eggs and bread. Sonnet ate quickly, mostly because he was starving. The provisions he'd packed paled in comparison to a freshly cooked meal. And Sandra had done well. The ugly woman was good for something. He wolfed down his eggs as she watched from across the room. When he was finished she came over, tugging down her low-cut blouse to expose her pale and pimply bosom.

'You want anything else, honey?' she said. 'I can warm you up right quick if you have a hankerin' for some loving.'

Sonnet looked into Sandra's face. Her red, unwashed hair hung in dirty curls over her brow. Her piggish nostrils flared and her blotched skin shone with a red rash.

'No thanks,' Sonnet said. 'You're a fine cook but I wouldn't love an ugly woman like you even with a lot of whiskey in my belly.'

'Why, you son of a bitch!' the woman screeched. 'You got no right to talk to me that way. Many a man has enjoyed my company. And you owe me two bits for the food.'

'I don't owe you a damn thing,' Sonnet said, rising from his seat. 'Your friends are going to make some good money off those saddles. That's the best deal this town has ever seen.'

He pushed through the batwing doors, ignoring Sandra's curses. The two men had removed the saddles from the wagon but were staring at Sonnet.

'You got a body in that coffin?' the barkeep asked.

'Not yet.'

'Who are you?' the other man asked.

'Chance Sonnet.'

'Jesus, Mary and Joseph!'

Sonnet climbed up on to the buckboard. He looked down at the two astonished men. 'I expect some riders might inquire about me,' he began. 'If that happens I'd be obliged if you'd ask them to reconsider their plans.'

'Reconsider their . . . their plans?' the man stammered.

'You heard me. Tell them I said dying is a whole lot easier than they think.'

Sonnet picked up the reins, unlatched the wheel brace and whistled at the horse. He rolled out of town with a full belly and ten dollars richer. He figured if he could stay alive he'd be a wealthy man before this was all over.

3

The tales had drifted across the West from the spring round-ups, across the copper telegraph wires, and in letters written by the light of oil lamps in hotels and from the homesteaders' ranches in the Dakotas. The name was spoken with awe, perhaps even reverence. It was a name that made the newspapermen from coast to coast put on their hats, leap from their chairs and make haste to the nearest saloon to compare notes with others of their trade.

The story had traveled south, sprung east, snaked back into the West in hushed tones. An aura of disbelief clung to the tale.

Chance Sonnet was alive!

It couldn't be true, but it was. At least, a man claiming to be Chance Sonnet was traveling south through

Nebraska. Two dead men lay in his wake. He rode on a buckboard carrying a pine coffin that he said was for Eric Cabot. Cabot, the son of the Kansas senator, Borland Cabot, told the Dodge City newspaper he had no idea why Chance Sonnet would be hounding him. Cabot said he never knew Sonnet, in fact, he doubted if the man was alive. It had to be a joke.

Others agreed. Sonnet was long dead. Killed in Missouri when he was hunting a gang of bank robbers. In Lincoln, Nebraska, the newspaperman Wallace Thimbleton rummaged through his old files and covered his desk with clippings and magazines. He found an old copy of *Harper's Monthly* magazine and thumbed through the yellowed pages. He studied the story for a good hour, reading it twice. The story was called *The Guns of Chance Sonnet*. The author was David Bridges, probably a pseudonym, but it was a great story. He recalled reading other stories about

Sonnet that seemed like exaggerations.

Thimbleton was engrossed in his reading when he felt a presence next to him. He looked up into the face of Jenny Connolly. Her beauty nearly took his breath away. Hired a year ago, the obligatory female to report on births, deaths, marriages and town gossip, Jenny had made herself indispensable with her dedication and talent. But sometimes the girl could be a nuisance. She was trying too hard to horn in on the newspaper's features. This was a man's world, but the girl just couldn't accept her place in society.

'Excuse me,' Jenny said, 'I couldn't help but notice you were looking over the clippings about Chance Sonnet.'

'We've had this discussion before,' Thimbleton said glumly.

'Oh no, it's not that. I know how you feel about my writing and all that, but I was just wondering if you'd heard anything.'

'Like what?' Thimbleton was perplexed.

Jenny placed herself firmly on the hard oak stool next to him. 'I heard two riders braced Sonnet at the Dakota border.'

'That's what they say. But what of it? The man's a killer.'

She studied him with those sparkling green eyes. 'I'm hearing on the street that Eric Cabot sent those men. Do you think there's any truth to that?'

Thimbleton set the magazine down. Beautiful or not, sometimes the girl asked the wrong questions.

'I heard that, too,' Thimbleton said. 'But it's his prerogative. The man has sworn to kill him. Cabot has the right to protect himself.'

'But that's not in the story you wrote.'

'No, of course not. The Cabot family can do what they damn well please. Some things aren't appropriate for print. And don't forget Cabot's father contributes a tidy sum to this paper.'

'But we don't even know why Sonnet wants to kill Cabot. It doesn't make sense not to ask. And isn't Cabot violating territorial law by sending his own gunman after Sonnet?'

Thimbleton nearly choked. 'Hot damn, girl! Are you daft? Don't let anyone outside of this office hear you talk like that. And it's not territorial law, it's state law, and Cabot's father is a senator.'

Jenny's brow furrowed. 'Mr Thimbleton, I believe everyone is missing the real story.'

'The real story?'

'Why does Chance Sonnet want Eric Cabot dead? What did Cabot do to bring this man out of hiding after fifteen years?'

Thimbleton thought it over before setting his stern gaze on Jenny. Their eyes locked. 'You're right, of course, that's the unknown part that makes it a good story. But what you need to understand is that this newspaper won't print a negative word about Eric Cabot. The Cabots are off limits. If you want to find out what grudge Sonnet has against Cabot you'll have to ask him. But I'm afraid you won't get the chance. It's unlikely that Chance Sonnet will live long enough to see Dodge City. Cabot's not about to let some crazy gunslinger get the better of him. Three more riders left yesterday. And Sonnet has other enemies. He put a lot of men in prison when he was a Texas Ranger, and by now everybody on the Plains knows what trail he's following.'

Jenny was silent a moment. 'Well, it's a shame. A story like that would be worth writing.' She rose to take her leave, but then as an afterthought she asked, 'Where do you suppose he is now?'

Thimbleton riffled through the papers on his desk, finally pulling out a yellowed map. He studied the map a moment and punched an arthritic finger at Nebraska.

'He should be about here,' Thimbleton said, 'Just shy of the Platte River. I would say he's a dead man before he makes the Kansas border.'

That afternoon Jenny made a decision that would change the course of her life. In her room at Ma Bump's boarding house, she packed a small valise with clothes. Then she counted her money. She had saved nearly every penny she'd earned in her life, sometimes sacrificing a good meal in order to save money. It was a foolish habit, she thought, but something in the back of her head kept her doing it. Now she was relieved that she had saved so much.

She had a copy of *Harper's Monthly* magazine that featured a story about Sonnet, and in the late afternoon light she read it again. There was a drawing of Sonnet but, of course, she had no way of knowing if the likeness was accurate: handsome with a strong chin; she was certain that if she met him his eyes would be softer than they appeared in the drawing. She decided it was a bad drawing.

The dime novel she had found at the dry-goods store, *Cavalier Tales*, had a story about Sonnet entitled *Gunfight at Massacre Ranch* by J.M. Bullock and it was, frankly, plain awful. The best information she had about Sonnet came from that magazine story, and from the pieces of gossip she'd picked up from Thimbleton. Men like to talk about other men they admire, and Jenny gathered that Thimbleton was a bit envious of Sonnet's reputation. That wasn't surprising considering that Thimbleton's life was entirely lacking in excitement.

And so was Jenny's. And she knew it.

She had for company the poetry of Lord Byron, John Keats and Percy Shelley. At twenty-six she was being called a spinster. The men who had courted her, like Lou Mahoney, were sincere but lacking in that spark she so fervently desired. It had taken a great deal of discussion to land the job working on the *Nebraskan Weekly*. Men didn't readily accept a woman holding a job other than school-teacher, which was her second career. Between teaching reading and arithmetic and working part-time for Thimbleton, she had little time for suitors. Her beauty, which nearly every man in town had noticed, assured her of regular callers. But now there was talk that she was too obsessed with her career. She was cold, they said, and distant.

The plan that blossomed in her mind was not one that most would have approved. Certainly, Thimbleton would never approve of such a plan, and that left her on her own.

She would track down Chance Sonnet and get his story. She would write it as a true story told by the man himself, and from this she expected recognition for all of her hard work.

It was a mad plan, but it filled her with excitement. She would leave by stage in the morning. Later, she would buy a horse. Riding was not a problem. She even had a small derringer in her valise. She could take care of herself. Jenny Connolly, spinster, newspaper-woman and school-teacher, was going to have herself an adventure.

4

Three days later the sky cleared and rain stopped. He awoke to a morning suffused with a strange glow as the sun broke free of the smoldering horizon. The land was bathed in an eerie, soft glow; the plains glistening with dew, the vegetation lush and green from all of the rain. The earth smelled pungent, alive with prairie flowers, thrumming with birdsong.

Sonnet had stopped near a sandy stretch of the Platte River and, perhaps sensing that trouble was brewing, decided to stay a day or two and fish the river. He used his Bowie knife and cut a fishing pole from a nearby sapling. The green wood was flexible and he was careful to carve the wood slowly, slicing away the small knobs and transforming the branch into a working tool. He had string in his saddle-bag and several thin iron hooks. He chose a hook and affixed it to the pole.

The damp earth was ripe with worms and he dug up a small patch, which attracted the robins and blue jays. With a worm squirming on his hook he tossed out an exploratory line. The strike was instantaneous but he lost the worm. No matter, he'd learned something. A successful fisherman knew when to be patient.

The river had a strong current; its banks were overflowing from the recent rain. He removed his boots and socks and waded into the river. The water was cold and his feet were instantly numb. Sonnet looked down into the green depths and saw the shadows of catfish glide past. He decided the current was too strong, and the fish were sweeping past too quickly. He needed to find a bend in the river, and a place where the shade from trees along the bank fell across the water.

He walked back to the wagon and checked the horse, then took a Colt from the coffin. He flipped open the loading gate and pulled the hammer back two clicks. Satisfied, he spun the cylinder so that the empty chamber once again rested under the hammer; he snapped the gate closed and eased the hammer down. He stuck the Colt in his belt. The Colt in his holster needn't be checked. He'd cleaned and oiled his own gun when the rain stopped. His instincts told him it was a two-gun day.

He looked down the river and chose a spot a quarter-mile away. There were plenty of trees and the sandbank had receded where the river zigzagged. He had a good eye for fishing, just like he had a good eye for shooting. It was a lifesaving skill that came to him naturally. Once again he waded into the water, this time up to his knees. Then he was perfectly still. Sonnet knew he had to 'become calm' which had been a technique his grandfather had taught him. *Just become calm and study on the water.* The years fell away and the old man's face came to him from that long-ago summer in southern Illinois. They were fishing on the Little Muddy, pulling out catfish and laughing. The memory faded and the cold water swirled past his numb legs; he tossed the line. The current wasn't as strong here but Sonnet let the line be swept out to his left. It curled back near the bank and the fish struck. He pulled the line but came up empty. But that was his spot, twenty yards down on his left.

He moved down the shore and pulled in his first fish ten minutes later. He caught four fish in thirty minutes and carried them back to the wagon. He made a fire and set to cleaning the fish. He sliced open the pale bellies and pulled out the entrails, tossing them casually along the riverbank. He made fillets from each fish and tossed the severed heads and tails on to the pile of gleaming entrails. Sonnet felt his stomach begin to rumble as he set the fillets in a pan and watched them begin to cook. He squatted by the fire just to enjoy the smell of fish cooking and the smell of pine twigs crackling in a fire.

As he ate he wondered why he was alive. The day's glorious bounty was nothing without his wife and son. The fever had taken them both. After that he had been inconsolable. He took his anger out on the outlaws he hunted. A year later he cornered a bank robber in San Antonio and shot him once in the belly. He watched the man writhe in pain, begging for a doctor, blood frothing on his lips as the internal hemorrhaging began. The man died with his eyes open and Sonnet had resigned from the Texas Rangers to become a bounty hunter.

The long years faded and birds chattered in the trees. Sonnet glanced up as a slight breeze brushed through the treetops. The sound of the trees swaying gently in a breeze was restful and he thought he might even take a nap while he was waiting. He finished the fish and wiped the pan clean with the last of his dried biscuits.

He returned the cleaned pan to the

wagon and then, still barefoot, he walked up a deer trail to a hilltop. He didn't have an ideal view but there was no sign of riders in any direction. But he knew they'd be here soon enough. The only question was how many? He figured three, maybe four. Cabot would be curious now, and worried.

He retrieved his boots and socks and pulled them on. Then he fetched a worn leather book from his saddle-bag and went to read under a tree. He propped himself next to the trunk with his legs outstretched and opened up *Oliver Twist* by Charles Dickens. Sonnet had learned to read when he was young and treasured whatever time he had to peruse books. Dickens was his favorite.

If he could have lived his life differently he might have been a teacher rather than a gunman. He'd read James Fenimore Cooper's novels and various dime novels, including a few that exploited his reputation. But nothing he'd read compared to Dickens. He had three books by Dickens in his saddle-bag.

He read for an hour, lost again in the London of long ago, and then he might have dozed, but when he blinked and looked up Lauren was walking toward him in the grass. She was barefoot and her blue-and-white cotton dress brushed the tips of daffodils and crocus as she skipped through the tall grass. She was smiling because in life her smile was unforgettable and there had never been a kinder girl of sixteen, so full of life, so gentle and beautiful. If his son had lived ... he choked at the thought, a solitary tear running down his cheek.

He had seen her this way once, dancing in the fields and pulling daisies from the grass and singing. How many times had she come to his carpentry shop and watched him work? From the time she was about seven, he thought, she had been there, especially in the summer.

Mister Neal! Mister Neal, can I

watch you work?

Carpentry fascinated the girl. She would stop by his shop and watch him carve chairs and tables from oak. He had a modest but successful business, the guns of his past finally behind him. One Christmas he fashioned a wooden doll for her, and a small boat. Her father, who had been ailing, thanked him for giving the girl a Christmas to remember. Her mother, who had died in childbirth, was truly blessing him from heaven.

She was the same age as his son, and if his son had lived he rather fancied he would have courted the girl. If he had lived . . .

Then the images in his dream were swept away like windblown leaves, only to be replaced by other ghosts. He dreamed about his wife and son, but the images were blurred, rushing past too quickly. He opened his eyes. The day was bright and warm but it was past noon and the afternoon shadows were beginning to pool under the trees.

The continuous flow of the river and the distant sound of a whippoorwill were all that he could hear.

He pulled himself to his feet, his mood foul. The ghosts still lingered on the periphery of his mind, a constant shadow that weighed him down with grief. If he could have expressed his emotions at that moment he would say that all of life was worthless and his grief was too much for one man to bear. This was no self-pity on his part, but rather a constant bewilderment and anguish.

For a while, as Frank Neal, he had managed to keep his grief in check. The work of a carpenter took all of his time and provided him with a kind of salvation against the darkness. But Lauren's death had brought it all back in a raging maelstrom, and then all he knew was vengeance.

Birds were pecking at the fish entrails. He slipped the Dickens into his saddle-bag and reconnoitered the area. There was still no sign of the riders he knew were coming. Tomorrow, then, he would engage them in another dance.

At sunset the raccoons appeared and feasted on the fish entrails. Two fat coons and finally a possum and a skunk appeared but by then the coons had eaten everything. He held himself in check when the skunk waddled near and sniffed at his boots. The skunks were the friendliest creatures but he had no desire to get sprayed.

The animals disappeared into the twilight and he made a fire and boiled coffee. He let his mind drift back to the years he spent practising with his Colt. His skill was so great, his aim unerring, that Bill Cody once proclaimed him the fastest gun alive. Sonnet had declined Cody's offer to join his Wild West show. He hadn't learned gunslinging to show off. When you're a Texas Ranger the gun is what keeps you out of the grave.

He wondered about Captain Will S. Walsh. Was he still alive? The man had been his closest friend during his service with the Rangers. He'd be close to sixty now, Sonnet reckoned. Walsh had implored him not to resign from the Rangers after Sonnet had killed that robber. The man had been wanted 'dead or alive' and no one would begrudge him the right to shoot the man, but Sonnet's grief was too much. By resigning from the Rangers he'd attempted to flee from his grief. He realized now, all these years later, that it hadn't worked. The darkness that surrounded him was unrelenting.

In the morning he again waded into the river, tossed his line and began pulling in catfish. He found it relaxing to watch the shadows of catfish strike at his line as the swirling green depths rushed past. The fish were plentiful and a plover and some small birds stood sentry duty on the shore. Today's catch would feed many birds and small animals.

He knew they were watching him as he cooked his lunch. He'd sensed them an hour earlier and had already prepared himself mentally. Three riders.

Lifting the frying pan he turned as they approached.

They were two grizzled old gunmen and a kid. The kid was cocky but rode a skittish horse.

'You're just in time for breakfast,' Sonnet said.

'Keep your hands away from those guns.'

'You can see my hands are full.'

'Are you Chance Sonnet?'

'I am.'

'Why are you gunning for Eric Cabot?'

'I'll tell him that just before I kill him.'

The three looked at each other. The kid spurred his horse and cantered around Sonnet. It was a good set-up. Two in front and one behind. They had him. Sonnet grinned.

'No sense in wasting this food.'

'We've got a proposition from Mr Cabot,' one of the men said.

Sonnet picked up a fork, crouched on his haunches and began eating.

'You listening to us?' the man asked.

'Sure, but I'm not gonna waste this food.'

'We got a thousand dollars in gold dust here. Call off your grudge and the gold is yours.'

'Only a thousand dollars?'

The man shifted uncomfortably on his horse. 'Mr Cabot said it's either you take the gold or you don't go any further. He says he doesn't even know you.'

'Let's gun him,' the kid behind him said.

Sonnet set the pan down and slowly brought himself to a standing position. Without their realizing it he'd altered his position so that the kid was closer to his right shoulder rather than being directly behind him.

'Listen boys,' Sonnet began, 'I've got a great idea. There's no sense in you dying.' The two men in front looked perplexed. 'You keep the gold. Cabot will be dead in a few weeks so he won't be asking for it back. All you have to do is lay low.'

After a moment the man on the left spat out a wad of chewing tobacco and fixed his eyes on Sonnet.

'Tarnation, mister! You're crazier than a loon. You've no place to go. We've got you set in a tight spot. You act as if you have a choice here.'

Sonnet looked at the man and silently counted to three. Then he shifted his gaze to a spot on the horizon between the two older horsemen. He stared ahead, knowing this shifting of his eyes would spook them. In his peripheral vision he saw them go for their guns. It was over quickly; in a blur of speed Sonnet's right hand pulled his Colt, the hammer thumbed back, the trigger engaged and the muzzle belching lead as his left hand tugged the second Colt from his belt. The second Colt barked and both men were tumbling from their saddles as Sonnet's right arm cocked, pointing his Colt over his right shoulder. He heard the kid's horse whinny as his Colt thundered.

Then he was turning in a crouch, but it was over.

His third bullet had shattered the kid's arm. He fell from the horse screaming. Sonnet darted forward and grabbed the reins. He stroked the horse's muzzle and held the reins tight until the animal relaxed.

The kid was crawling on the ground, desperately trying to reach his fallen Peacemaker.

'Leave it be and I'll tend to your wound,' Sonnet said.

The kid's eyes filled with tears. Sonnet knew the pain was nearly unendurable.

'I . . . I . . . never seen anyone . . . shoot so fast . . . you shot me over your shoulder . . . like a trick shooter . . . in a circus.'

The bullet had torn away bone and muscle on the kid's right elbow. It was his gun arm. He would be maimed for life.

'Kid, your shootin' days are over. But you'll live. I reckon you earned that thousand dollars. It's all I can do for you.'

The kid's name was Toby Grapewin. Sonnet's immediate concern was in stanching the blood flow so the kid didn't bleed to death. He stitched the wound with his fishing line. With Toby propped against a tree, Sonnet set to stripping the two dead men of their weapons. Their saddle-bags were heavy with beef jerky and ammunition, and Sonnet acquired two more saddles.

Toby had lost a lot of blood but Sonnet thought he'd live as long as the infection wasn't bad. That was always the unknown factor, although he wouldn't tell the kid. Sonnet had ample experience with gunshot wounds. The fever would begin tomorrow. Then the kid would have two difficult days and either recover or die. Sonnet was betting Toby would live. He was young and strong and presumably stubborn enough to walk away from this.

Having no sympathy for hired guns, Sonnet would normally leave them for

49

the vultures. With Toby laid up for a day or two the bodies would not only begin to smell, but they would attract coyotes and other carnivores. Sonnet carried each body a half-mile downstream and released the bodies into the current. Sonnet easily lifted the bodies. His forearms and shoulders were sinewy from years of carpentry work. The Platte River was brimming from the spring thaw and the bodies would travel a long distance before the fish and nature turned them into a pile of bones.

By mid-afternoon Toby was sleeping fitfully. An occasional moan would escape his lips and he tossed back and forth, but the movement must have sent sparks of pain along his arm. Then he would cry out before settling back into an uneasy slumber.

Sonnet felt sympathy for the boy. The kid appeared intelligent and should have known better than to get mixed up with gunslingers. Too many of these young kids had read those dime novels and magazine stories glorifying the

West. Now they all wanted to be like Wild Bill Hickok. It didn't matter that Hickok's reputation served no purpose other than securing him a place six feet deep in a hill in Deadwood.

When Toby woke up after sundown Sonnet gave him some coffee.

'That tastes good,' Toby said. His mouth was dry and he sipped at the coffee greedily.

'You've got to keep liquids in you from here on out,' Sonnet said. 'You can't get dehydrated. You'll lose your strength that way. Water, coffee or even whiskey, but only a little whiskey. You're a tad young to be drinking whiskey.'

'I've had whiskey before,' Toby said weakly. 'Can't say that I really cared for it.'

'It's best that you don't get a taste for it.'

They were quiet a moment, watching the yellow flames dance along the logs Sonnet had used to build his fire.

'Where you from?' Sonnet eventually asked.

'Dodge.'

'Been there.' Sonnet said. 'A long time ago. How did you get mixed up with Cabot?'

'He has the money in town. Heard that his pa's a senator.'

'You thought being a gunfighter would make you rich?'

'It wasn't like that at first. I needed the money, is all. I've never been in a gunfight.' Toby set his coffee down and looked at Sonnet. 'Mister, I'm sorry about all this. I regret the day I took Cabot's money and picked up a gun.' Tears welled in his eyes and Sonnet looked away.

A minute later he said without looking up, 'You can have the money I pulled from their pockets and saddle-bags. That sets you up with three thousand dollars. Don't go bragging about it. And that arm won't be much use for a long while. Maybe it won't be much use at all.'

'You mean I'll be a cripple?'

'Not a cripple. That's a man that

can't fend for himself. But I expect that arm won't be exactly right again.' Sonnet paused. The flames licked at the logs and the fire crackled. 'Hell, kid, you're lucky to be alive. You got family?'

'Got a sister works as a fancy girl at the Longbranch saloon. She's no good.'

'What about your ma and pa?'

'Never knew my pa. My ma died about a year ago. I took a job mopping up saloons to feed myself. Then about a week ago Cabot offered this money . . . ' His voice trailed off.

It was an all too familiar story. Toby was one of the increasing number of boys born into the world without a proper family. Without the guidance of a strong mother and father his chances of doing something good with his life were small. Sonnet winced. The prairie was crowded with drifting kids like Toby. Too many of them ended up in unmarked graves or doing long stints in territorial prisons.

'You know how to read?'

Toby looked up, a puzzled expression

on his face. 'Sure, I can read a little. Haven't seen a book in years. My ma used to read to me from the Bible.'

Sonnet went to his saddle-bag in the buckboard and pulled out *Oliver Twist*. He handed the book to Toby. 'If you can prop that open with one hand you might find this is a good book. Maybe it'll help pass the time.'

Sonnet wanted to tell Toby that books are another way of learning that can help set a man's course in the right direction but he feared he would sound like a preacher. Toby managed to balance the book on his knees and thumb through the pages.

'I'm obliged.'

After awhile Toby looked up from the book and asked, 'Why do you want Cabot dead?'

'Everybody keeps asking me that question,' Sonnet replied.

'You gonna tell me?'

'No.'

'He must have done something bad for you to want him dead.'

'I'll tell him when I see him.'

'I think he'll try to kill you first.'

'That's been his plan. Doesn't seem to be working, does it?'

An owl hooted in the distance. The fire had burned low and Sonnet added some branches and another log.

'I heard stories about you. They said you protected a whore that was accused of slitting a man's throat.'

'True enough.'

'Did she do it?'

'She did. Found out later she was guilty as hell. They hanged her. Not many women get hanged.'

'So why did you protect her?'

'The law says a person is innocent until a trial proves them guilty. They have to be judged by the law, not a mob of angry people. She got beat by a respected man and she killed him for it. I wouldn't let his brothers touch her until they had a trial.'

'So you protected her for no good reason?'

'I protected her because it was the

right thing to do. And when they hung her it was the right thing to do.'

'And going after Cabot, if that's right then why aren't any lawmen after him?'

'This isn't about the law.'

'Then what's it about? You don't make sense.'

Sonnet frowned. The kid asked a lot of questions. 'I reckon I'll explain it all to Cabot just before I shoot him.'

'I think you're a complicated man,' Toby said.

'I expect so.'

5

Captain William Samuelson Walsh had been enjoying his retirement until he read the paper that morning. He had a modest ranch with a decent herd of cattle, a gentle wife, and a son out East studying to be a lawyer. He had money in the bank. Texas was good enough for him. The desire to see other parts of this grand country had been satiated in his youth and his years with the Texas Rangers had provided him with all the stories his future grandchildren would need. Now that was all changed.

Chance Sonnet was alive and Walsh had an obligation to fulfill. After reading the paper he sat quietly in a leather-backed chair in his den and smoked a thin cigar. He absent-mindedly stroked his handlebar mustache as he recalled the brash young Ranger he'd befriended all those years ago. Sonnet's life had turned tragic. He'd never come to grips with the death of his wife and son who had died from the fever within days of each other. Hell, Walsh didn't think any man deserved to have that much grief visited upon him, but life in the West was often cruel.

Sonnet had become a bounty hunter, driven by anger. He'd tracked only men who were wanted 'dead or alive'. Sonnet had never brought any of them in alive. Walsh mourned for his friend as his legend grew. Then he'd heard that Sonnet perished along the Missouri River in a furious gunfight with three hardened robbers. The robbers had died but witnesses from the sheriff's office reported Sonnet had been wounded and fallen into the river, in which his body had been swept away by the strong current.

Over the years Walsh had wondered about those reports, but no evidence had materialized that Sonnet had survived. And no body had been found. Now the newspapers were crackling with tales of his reappearance.

Walsh went to an oak bookcase and rummaged through books and papers until he found some old territorial maps. The maps were outdated, but he wanted to estimate the distance he would travel. He could do most of it by train, but he didn't think he could get to Dodge City in time. He would go north through Oklahoma and then into south-eastern Kansas. From there he would switch trains before traveling into Dodge City.

As far as he could tell from the newspaper stories, Sonnet hadn't broken any laws. The bodies of several hired guns had been found along the route Sonnet was traveling, but Walsh knew Sonnet would let the gunmen draw first. That made it self-defense.

He turned his mind to Eric Cabot. The man had no criminal record, only a reputation for being a scoundrel. Whatever the man had done it had brought Chance Sonnet out of hiding. Walsh wanted to make certain that

Sonnet didn't cross that sometimes thin line between justice and vengeance. He had to talk with Sonnet. He owed him that.

He stubbed out his cigar. No sense wasting time. He strapped on his gunbelt and stomped out to tell his wife the news.

Two days later he was camped in northern Oklahoma and listening to some cowpunchers share the news they'd picked up in a Dodge City saloon. Walsh had kept his horse in a carriage car on the train for an extra ten dollars, but decided to get off the train when the passenger gossip led him to believe that Sonnet was near by. He decided to pick up the trail on horseback. With the train's smokestack belching black smoke that trailed off into the distant blue horizon, Walsh waited until the train was a speck in the distance before spurring the horse he'd brought along a fresh cattle trail.

The following morning he'd connected with a small herd being coaxed up toward Dodge. The cowpunchers invited him for grub, more than a little curious to learn why he was riding lonesome when such a notorious outlaw as Chance Sonnet was on the loose.

'He's not an outlaw,' Walsh said. 'He hasn't broken any laws.'

Slim MacDougal, the foreman of the group, squinted at Walsh through a blue cloud of cigarette smoke. 'You sound like you might know something about this fella.'

'We rode together a long time ago when we were with the Rangers.'

'You're a Texas Ranger?'

'Retired. I'm looking for Sonnet to find out what this is about.'

'Is that so? You ever meet gunslingers like Hank Benteen or Maxfield Knight?'

Walsh shook his head. 'Nope. Hell, this is a mighty big country. You can get lost in an arroyo and drown in a flash flood just as quick. I might ride past Wyatt Earp without knowing who he is.'

'Well, this Sonnet has killed a lot of

men. South of here about seventy-five miles is a town called Burkeville, and he killed two there.'

'Have you or any of your men seen him?'

'Nope. Found his camp. Saw the buckboard trail. They say he's hauling a pine coffin for the senator's son. Now why would he want to kill Cabot?'

'That's the question I intend on asking him.'

Walsh finished his grub and stood, stretching his tired calf muscles. Mac-Dougal stood and Walsh tipped his hat. 'I'm obliged for the grub.'

'Sure, pard. Say, there's one more thing I heard. There's a woman tailing him. Some schoolmarm.'

'A schoolmarm?'

'Yep, heard she has fair skin and a figure that'll keep a man awake. She's riding an old paint. Those buckboard tracks should make finding Chance Sonnet easy enough, and you'll probably see her horse's tracks right alongside.'

'Good to know.'

Walsh considered his options. He was south of Dodge City and might just wait for Sonnet to make an appearance. Sonnet, coming down from the north, would be under constant attack from Cabot's men. He would have to change his route. Traveling by buckboard made him far too easy to track. Of course, Sonnet knew this and Walsh wondered if he cared. It seemed foolish to him.

He was but a few hours' ride from the Kansas border. Although most of Kansas was flat, eastern Kansas had many hills and small valleys, and the territory was marked by dozens of rivers, streams and creeks. Sonnet would constantly be crossing water on his way to Dodge City. The flat landscape was deceptive; hills and forests and rivers offered sanctuary where any capable man could hide. Thus far, Sonnet had not taken any evasive action. He was plunging south in a straight line. Walsh decided to go after him rather than wait in Dodge.

Pulling himself into the saddle, he spurred his horse into a leisurely canter. He had to admit it felt good to be out in the open, riding under a cloudless blue sky, the warm wind nudging him along. Maybe this was just what he needed. Hell, he had wondered recently if he was getting soft in his old age. That leather chair was a nice place to relax in the evening. A fire glowing in the hearth and a book to read had become his daily routine. He hadn't fired a gun in over three years. His ranch hands did all the hunting, and they had beeves to slaughter, so they were never shy of meat for the table.

And there was something else too, something that he wouldn't admit openly. *Once a lawman always a lawman*. Sure, he had put his life on the line many times, but what mattered most was seeing outlaws in jail, or even seeing them hang. He had done his part, and he had enjoyed every moment on the long trail. Captain Walsh had no regrets.

But Chance Sonnet's fate had long plagued him. When he first heard that he had died in Missouri he was skeptical. That wasn't right by a long shot. Sonnet wouldn't be taken in a fight like that. He was too canny. As the years drifted past he often thought of Sonnet and hoped that if, by some miracle, he was alive then Walsh prayed that Sonnet had found a measure of peace. What he had endured would break the stoutest man's heart. Losing a wife and son so quickly had broken him.

That brought Captain Walsh to the obvious question. Now that everyone knew that Sonnet was alive, what had Eric Cabot done to provoke his anger? That was the question he intended to ask his old friend. Walsh had asked around, and Cabot was well known as a ladies' man, a drunk and a braggart, but as far as anyone knew, he had not broken any laws. But Chance Sonnet had sent advance word that he intended killing Cabot, and Sonnet himself had made the pine coffin he was bringing for Cabot's body. The boldness of these statements burst like a thunderbolt across the prairie.

He camped in a grove of gnarly oaks, his campfire set between the two tallest trees. He estimated he was but five miles from Dodge City. He made camp at twilight, just at that moment when the landscape began to darken and the light was like a fragile blue veil waving on the horizon. Against the pale light the oak branches clawed at the sky, the leaves chattering anxiously.

He heard a horse nicker, the rattle of conchos, the creak of old leather. Three riders emerged from the prairie mist, heralds of doom under Cabot's direction. They remained on horseback, spread out and surrounding the camp. Walsh looked at the closest rider, his Colt immediately in his hand.

'You boys got me jumping. What do you want?'

'Who are you?'

'Captain Walsh, retired Texas Ranger.

I'm on my way north to visit an old friend.'

'You seen anybody on the trail?'

Walsh holstered his gun. 'Cowpunchers south of here. You boys happen to be looking for Chance Sonnet? I heard about him. They say he's bringing a coffin to Dodge.'

A nervous silence, a phlegmy cough. 'We work for Mr Cabot. Have you seen any sign of this Sonnet?'

'Nope, not a bit. Say, what did this Cabot do to get Sonnet all riled up?'

'It don't matter,' the man said. 'He won't get to Dodge.'

'Is that right? Well, so far I heard he's done a good job getting into Kansas.'

'We're gonna look around.'

They circled the camp and then dismounted. All three men had Winchesters in their hands, and Walsh noted with amusement that they never lost sight of where he was standing. So he remained fixed in one spot, not making any sudden moves. He might have mentioned there were no obvious signs of a buckboard anywhere near here, but he opted for silence. Some boys were brighter than others, and thus far Cabot didn't appear to associate with known geniuses.

When they were finished looking the man said, 'If we find out you lied we'll come looking for you.'

Walsh raised an eyebrow. 'Lied? I said I was going north to visit an old friend. You can send a telegram to the San Antonio Texas Rangers office to verify my name. I wouldn't waste my time lying to a pipsqueak like you.'

The men backed up their horses, turned, and slid into the twilight. Walsh watched them for a few minutes. They undoubtedly had a camp near by, and at least one of them would immediately report back to Cabot.

As night fell Captain Walsh drank a cup of Arbuckle's coffee and wondered again what Cabot had done. Whatever it was, he'd bet a bucket of silver dollars that Chance Sonnet was going to do exactly what he said he'd do.

6

Toby Grapewin was lost in London. He had never been to a city bigger than Dodge City, and the idea excited him. A place with tall buildings with smokestacks and girls in colorful dresses. He wondered if all of the wealthy kings of England read books as good as *Oliver Twist*.

'You got any other books?'

Sonnet looked at him. 'You haven't finished that one yet.'

'But I will and then I'll need more. I like reading. This Fagin fellow is like Cabot.'

'I suppose so. I hadn't thought of it until you mentioned it.'

'If Oliver Twist can stop being a thief he might make something of himself. I guess you wanted me to read this book because it's about people like me.'

'Hell, kid I'm not that smart. I just gave you that book to read because it's a good book. I have a few more you can read when you're finished with that one.'

'Sure.'

Sonnet knew that the after-effects from a bullet wound might result in fever and chills. The body takes a shock from a bullet and then an infection sets in. Toby's wound wasn't fatal. But Sonnet waited to see how sick the kid would get. It would be like his body had suddenly awakened to the realization that it was hurt.

When Toby wasn't reading he slept. He did not sleep easily. The pain was constant and it clouded his mind. Still, Sonnet was impressed that he could concentrate on reading. Any bullet wound that shattered bone would hurt like hell, and for a long time. Sonnet had taken a hit once on his leg and sometimes, especially when the weather turned cold, it would hurt all over again.

Toby defied expectations and suffered only from the pain, which was enough. No fever plagued him. Sonnet saw that as a good sign. The flesh around his wound was puffy and red so he made a poultice from moss, mud and prairie grass. He had wrapped the wound in a bandanna, and after washing the bandanna in a creek he let it dry in the sun before re-wrapping the wound.

He worried that remaining in one spot too long made them easier targets. Cabot would have more men about searching for him. Sonnet moved their camp east and set it low in a ruffle of hills and meandering trees. The nearby river and adjoining creeks would provide them with fish, and he could set snares to catch rabbits. He made the snares from twine and branches that he cut, having learned to make a rabbit snare from his father. He showed Toby how to make the snares, explaining that it was a good practice to learn things that put food in front of you.

Then the weather changed. He saw it in the sky, a darkening at the horizon. The blue sky gave way to lavender; the somber clouds began to gather in the distance like an army of black riders. The air seemed to gather an intensity. The lonely, hard country was like a thing possessed, building momentum. The warm breeze smelled of rain, and then it did not smell of rain. The wildflowers and tall prairie grass began to rustle in the ominous breeze. Voices came with the breeze and Toby asked if those were the spirits of the Sioux talking to them. Sonnet was at a loss for words. He studied the sky.

A thousand trees stretched to the horizon, spread out over the green-and-brown swell of rolling grasslands. The summer had already provided more rain than in previous years, and the lush landscape was ripe, alive with birds and insects and small animals foraging for food. The dark clouds billowing in their direction sucked all sound out of the air and an eerie silence descended over the world. Once again he smelled rain, and far in the distance a purple wall with rain slanting through it and sparkling with lightning sent the first cannonade of thunder.

Something changed in the clouds, higher even than the mountains of Wyoming or Colorado, a towering mass of blistering clouds that seemed to weep tears of blood. It was a dizzying sight, and Sonnet felt a hollow pit in his stomach. There was nowhere to hide. South-east of them a speck caught his attention. It was a lone rider, a small indistinct figure riding in their direction. It would take the rider an hour to reach them, and soon thereafter the storm would strike. What bothered him the most were the funnel clouds that began to strike at the fertile land like airborne serpents.

He set to the task of securing the wagon. He took it down near the river, secluded in a depression just feet from the river's edge, in a spot lower than the prairie. Then he unharnessed the horse and hobbled one leg with a length of rope tied to a brick. The horse could move and graze freely but wouldn't be able to gallop far. He knew the horse would buck in fear shortly and try to get away. Without the horse he was stranded. He was gambling that the horse — that all of them — would survive.

An hour could be an eternity under certain conditions, or could appear to pass in moments. When he next glanced up at the sky the storm towered over them like a dark behemoth.

The rider was closer and now he could make out the figure. It was a woman on horseback. Thunder boomed closer and the smell of rain assailed him. The wind had picked up. The air tore at him, pleading, pulling him away. The rider had not seen him, so he raised his arms and shouted. She lifted her head and saw him.

A funnel cloud twisted across the prairie, debris smashing up from its tip — trees and brush and small bits of fence spun crazily in the air. The woman on horseback galloped toward him.

When she was ten feet away she halted and stared at Sonnet incredulously.

'Get off your horse!' he bellowed.

'Are you . . . ?'

'Get off your horse! We don't have much time!'

As she slid from the horse he was unbuckling the saddle. 'Follow me. Bring the horse.'

They descended the sloping hill and entered the underbrush that bordered the river. Sonnet brought her saddle and blanket and tossed them into the buckboard.

'I don't have any way to hobble your horse,' he said, 'so she'll run. We might get lucky and find her later.' Toby was crouched down near the buckboard wheel. 'I want you under the buckboard.'

The wind was screaming like a banshee and for the first time he paused and looked at the woman. Her chestnut hair was tangled from the wind and she tried futilely to push her hair away from her face, her bright eyes staring at him in amazement. Her simple beauty took him by surprise and left him breathless. The girl was speechless herself, her cheeks flushed red as she stared back at him.

Regaining his composure, Sonnet asked, 'Who are you?'

Blinking, her lips moving but making no sound, he thought she was embarrassed.

'Jenny. Jenny Connolly.' Her eyes swept over the buckboard with its pine coffin. 'I came here looking for you, Mr Sonnet.' She had immediately realized who he was.

'You're not the only one looking for me.' he said quickly. 'We have to get under the buckboard. There's no place else. Look!'

The tornado ripped through a grove of trees, the limbs sheared off as if they were paper, the tree trunks uprooted as if plucked from the earth by a giant. It was a fearsome sight: a long twisting mass of dirt and clouds grabbing and destroying everything in its path. The tornado would pass very close to them.

He pulled Jenny by the arm and they crouched low, huddled beneath the buckboard. The wind found them and attempted to lift the buckboard. Sonnet knew that if it were not set in the low area he had chosen the wind would surely have lifted the buckboard. They were just low enough, tucked below a ridgeline, to escape the wind's full strength.

The air screamed and the world around them was destroyed. They could not see five feet in front of them. The wind was a demon that spat a harsh venom; the horrific neighing of the horses caught their ears, and then all they heard were the crackling sounds of trees and soil torn apart, dirt and branches hurtling around the buck-board. Sonnet had a glimpse of Toby. He had taken the book and slipped it under his shirt, holding it close to his chest. Remarkably, in the midst of chaos, Sonnet found himself thinking: *That book belongs to the boy now.* A tree crashed against the buckboard and the girl screamed. Without thinking he put his arms around her for comfort and she leaned closer, shivering in fear.

Suddenly the screaming wind ceased and the rain came down in tumults. Sonnet breathed a sigh of relief at the sound of rain. They had survived the worst of it, and when the rain ceased he could find the horses. The air had briefly turned cold, but at length the rain lessened and the air became muggy, ripe with the scent of soil.

Crawling from beneath the buckboard, they peered at their camp. The tornado had missed them by only a few feet. The camp was obliterated. A small tree had fallen across the buckboard, and it took some minutes before Sonnet could lever himself into position to move it. A section of the buckboard had been damaged, but the coffin and its contents of guns were unharmed. Sonnet's horse was near by, also unharmed but skittish. They could not find Jenny's horse.

Toby, kicking through a debris field of wind-tossed branches, found the coffee pot that had rested atop their campfire. Ultimately, they had lost nothing, having barely escaped with their lives, and Sonnet was forced to turn his attention to the girl.

'Your horse might still show up,' he said lamely, 'but until then you'll have to ride with us. I'll take you to the nearest town or see you safely to a ranch.'

'I can't thank you enough, Mr Sonnet. I am truly indebted to you.'

'Now what's this about you looking for me?' he asked. 'I have enough trouble as it is.' Sonnet would not have thought it was possible for Jenny to blush a deeper shade of red, but she did.

'Why, I work for the *Nebraskan Weekly* and I would like to write a story about you.'

'A story? You work for a newspaper?'

'Yes, that's what I said. I suppose you think it's unusual for a woman to be working for a newspaper, but let me assure you, Mr Sonnet, that I have as equal a right to work as any man, and . . . '

Sonnet burst out laughing. 'That's the dandiest thing I've ever heard! I'm being chased all over the country by killers who work for Eric Cabot and a newspaperwoman finds me in a tornado!'

Toby, moving up for a closer look at Jenny, was grinning.

'And who is this young man?' Jenny demanded, her feathers slightly ruffled.

'I'm Toby.'

'What happened to your arm?'

'Mr Sonnet here shot me. I was hired by Mr Cabot with some other men to gun him. They all died except me.'

Jenny turned white.

'Listen,' Sonnet interjected, 'we need to keep an eye on things and get you to safety. You can write all you want after I disappear again.'

'So you plan on killing Cabot and then going into hiding again? I'm not trying to offend you. I just want to know what this is all about.'

'Later. Look at the sky.' Sonnet pointed over her shoulder.

The sky was green. They had an unobstructed view of the prairie stretching all the way to Colorado. Far in the distance another mass of dark clouds filled the horizon. To the north several small funnel clouds whipped at the earth.

'I thought the storm was over.'

'Kansas is like that. Tornadoes all damn summer sometimes. Those tornadoes are coming in from the north-west, so we're going south-west.'

Sonnet hitched his horse to the buckboard and pulled up from the river. The three of them crowded on to the buckboard seat. Jenny, glancing back at the coffin, saw that the lid had come loose.

'Why are those guns in the coffin? Do

outlaws need that many guns to kill one man?'

'Outlaws?'

He snapped the reins and they started south at a westerly angle. An uneasy silence descended on them and Sonnet concentrated on the trail, a wary eye on the storm that was brewing in the north-west. Eventually, Jenny chatted with Toby, and Toby told her about *Oliver Twist*. Jenny had read *A Tale of Two Cities*, and Sonnet mentioned that he had a beat-up copy in his saddle-bag. Late that afternoon they had arrived at a creek in an area of rolling hills and oaks and maple trees. Sonnet brought the buckboard into the trees, and they made camp.

The sun had broken free of the clouds and meadow larks sang pleasantly in the distance. Far to the east the storm loomed like a bully on the otherwise clear horizon. Sonnet reckoned the storm was hitting Dodge City.

An hour later he had pulled some fish from the creek and Jenny helped him clean them before cooking them. He was impressed at how quickly she worked. She used some of Sonnet's flour supply and made crude biscuits in the pan. After eating the fish and biscuits, she took the pan and Sonnet's knife and fork and cleaned them downstream. She made coffee and they sat around the campfire talking. Toby was eager to talk, and he told Jenny all about Eric Cabot, and again how Sonnet had shot him, but had then saved him from bleeding to death. Sonnet thought the way the kid was saying it made it sound as if Sonnet had done a great thing.

'I just did what was logical,' he interjected. 'My father would have called it common sense for country folk.'

'Your father sounds like a wise man,' Jenny said.

'Aw, hell!' Sonnet was suddenly at a loss for words. He stood up and went to check on the horse. He thought they had good cover and they might wait a day here to see if any further storms drifted in. Kansas storms all happened quickly, with little warning. They were lucky to have survived that close encounter with a tornado.

Standing on the periphery of their camp, he looked east and saw the distant flash of lightning in a mountain of purple clouds. The storm had moved east and past Dodge City. Darkness fell quickly. Toby and Jenny sat huddled around the campfire in the growing darkness, both of them with their hands around their knees, not from the cold, certainly, because it was a humid evening; but Sonnet thought they both appeared at ease and comfortable.

He brought a small bundle of firewood he'd gathereed up and set it down. Hunkering at the fire, they talked of unimportant matters — the price of beef, the style of clothing Jenny had seen in a Sears Roebuck catalog — and when Toby curled up later under a horse blanket he waited for Jenny to ask her questions.

'Are you going to tell me what this is all about?'

'You don't belong here.' he responded, but when he looked at her, the firelight shining in her face, her skin soft, her eyes warm, he felt just the opposite.

'But here I am. I came all this way because of you. Why did you take offense when I referred to you as an outlaw?'

'I'm not an outlaw.'

'Explain to me what kind of man you are. Surely you want the truth known. You might have remained hidden under an assumed name for ever. What brought you out of hiding?'

Sonnet sighed. What harm would it do to tell her? Besides, he might fail. Cabot could succeed in stopping him.

'There was a girl,' he began slowly, 'a young girl who died. Cabot was responsible for her death. He didn't kill her himself, but it was the same as if he had. That's why I'm after him.'

'I don't understand. This girl, was she . . . your lover?'

'No, no, nothing like that.' His voice had taken a softer tone. 'She was sixteen, just a kid. She watched me work in my shop. I worked as a carpenter. She had little habits . . . little things she did that made me smile.' His eyes had a faraway look and Jenny thought he was finished talking, but then his fingers tugged nervously at his tobacco pouch and he rolled himself a cheroot.

'When my son was two he had golden hair like his mother. Sometimes when I watched him I could see him growing. It was like I could see all of the mystery of the world before him and I saw how his mind was learning to fit things together.' Sonnet paused and glanced self-consciously at Jenny. 'I'm not a religious man, but it was like watching a miracle.'

'I know that you loved them very much . . . ' Jenny wanted him to continue. 'I read they had died of fever.' She was mesmerized. She had never heard a man talk with such sensitivity before. His grief was palpable.

'My wife had a way of tossing her head to shake her hair from her eyes. Lauren, that was the girl's name. I went by the name of Frank Neal. Lauren had that same habit of shaking her hair from her eyes. She reminded me of my wife, but only a little. She was just a pleasant kid.'

Sonnet smoked and watched the campfire, his eyes shining.

'What happened to the girl?' Then for a moment Jenny thought she shouldn't have asked, but there it was, her words filled the silence that hung between them. Sonnet's face hardened.

'Eric Cabot came to town. She was taken with him. Cabot strikes a woman's fancy. He talks real smooth, but I could see through him. Lauren liked him a little too much, I guess, and girls can get foolish notions just like young boys. I told her once to be careful, but she just laughed. Damn, she was a sweet kid . . . ' he paused, his eyes misting over. 'Anyway, about four months after Cabot vamoosed Lauren found out she was going to have a baby.'

Jenny felt a shock run through her.

'She was just a kid, and to be shamed like that. I guess it was too much. She hanged herself in her father's barn.'

Jenny was stunned. Now she understood Chance Sonnet's trek across the plains, and a chill went down her spine.

'Oh my god! Surely the law . . . ?'

'No.'

'There must be some lawman . . . ?'

'Cabot's father took care of that with money. I know the law. I wore the badge of a Texas Ranger, but this isn't about the law any longer. And I damn well know nothing will bring her back, so it's not even justice. The pain stays. It becomes a part of life itself.'

'Then what? What is this about?'

When Sonnet looked at Jenny there were tears in his eyes. 'Accountability. That's a big word that means doing the right thing. I think about Lauren, and the promise she had, and somebody has to speak for her.' Sonnet glanced back at the sleeping form of Toby Grapewin. 'And him, too. I might have killed that boy, but now he has a chance. That arm won't be much use, but he has his life.'

'What does killing Eric Cabot prove?'

Again silence filled the dark void between them. After a while Sonnet said, 'Maybe it'll just give me satisfaction.' Then he was on his feet and without another word he strode into the darkness.

Jenny watched his form blend into the night and she shivered.

7

Eric Cabot stood on the porch of his father's ranch five miles south of Dodge City and watched the storm tumble in his direction, a sense of foreboding and oppression clinging to him with the irritating persistence of a damp shirt. For two weeks now this man Chance Sonnet had eluded assassination by his best men. Word had reached him before Sonnet had left the Dakota territory. Not knowing precisely what act of his, real or imagined, had provoked the legendary gunman out of hiding only added to his feeling of powerlessness. He had racked his brain trying to recall some insult to some lone cowpoke, something that would shed light on his death sentence, but there was nothing.

Eric Cabot was, by his own estimation, a fine fellow. He also accepted without apology that he was not a saint.

No, Eric Cabot was very much his father's son, and therefore just as deadly. He had killed his first man at fifteen: a drunk in Wichita. His father's influence had hushed up the incident, and there were no ramifications. His temper had been the cause of that killing, and he thought idly that perhaps he had made a mistake after all. Perhaps some relative of some deceased wastrel had connected him to one of the five men he had killed, although that didn't appear likely.

Only Chance Sonnet could say for certain what his grudge was about. Cabot decided to change tactics. His foreman, Lacey, was coming out of the bunkhouse and Cabot waved him over. Lacey was short, no more than five feet and two inches, but tough as any wrangler. His black beard glittered with sweat.

'Where do we have the big Swede working?'

'Halvar? He's riding fence.'

Cabot was thoughtful a moment.

'Get him. I have a proposition for him.'

'You know he doesn't like guns.' Lacey said. 'He won't do it.'

Cabot glared at Lacey. 'Don't presume to read my mind. Get the Swede.'

With Lacey gone, Cabot entered the house and seated himself in his den at a large custom-made oak desk. His father's money had made this ranch possible, and Cabot had made his father proud with his profitable cattle business. Eric Cabot may have been a murderer and philanderer, but he wasn't lazy. The double C brand was not only profitable, but respected for its fair dealings. It may well have been Eric's only honest activity, born from the need to both please his father and keep the old man at arm's length.

He poured a tumblerful of whiskey, sipped the drink and leaned his elbows on the desk, deep in thought. Chance Sonnet had become an obsession. Cabot was convinced that he never met the man. The stories drifting back to him indicated that Sonnet had appeared in the Dakotas when he pronounced his death sentence against him. Cabot had business dealings all over the Dakotas, but he couldn't place having met anyone matching Sonnet's description, nor could he recall having any altercation that might stimulate such an act of vengeance. He was puzzled.

His habit on such business trips had been to seek out some pretty girl to romance, and then politely leave town. The girls made for a nice diversion, and there had never been any serious entanglements. Then he recalled one young girl about six months ago. His father had wired him that some complaint had been filed, but for the life of him Eric Cabot couldn't recall the girl's name. There had been too many such diversions to keep track of. Was it possible this girl was the cause of the trouble? He had to admit it was a possibility, but he couldn't recall any further details. The big Swede might prove to be useful. He needed Sonnet to be in a place where he could be controlled. The Swede was good at controlling people when he put his mind to it.

Eric Cabot was not a superstitious man. He was far too vain and self-centered to care at all about superstitions or myths. In fact, lost to him then that day was the significance of the sky's color. The colors had special significance depending on who was telling of its importance. The Sioux undoubtedly had many tales about a sky such as this one; streaked with red at the horizon. The wind brought something with it from the sky; an unholy taste and smell, not entirely of this earth. Only an individual with acute senses might notice such details. Eric Cabot had no way of knowing that all of the signs about him were bad omens. The thought of running never crossed his mind. Once he had a plan — to bring the Swede into it — he was content.

When he was twenty he found

himself one night in a St Louis saloon playing poker with some yokels who irritated him with their smug manner. He lost heavily that night — 500 dollars — and the man who won the pot was marked. He wore a fancy string tie and a bowler hat that made him look dandified. He even wore gold cufflinks. Cabot was clever in planning his vengeance. Before he left St Louis he made a point of learning where the man worked and lived. Then Cabot left town and even wished them all luck saying he might come back next spring to try and win some of that money back.

Five days later Cabot was in St Louis again, but across town under a different name. It was a one-night stop. He waited for the man to emerge from that same saloon late at night, and when the opportunity presented itself he struck. He slowly choked the man to death. The feeling of absolute power was intoxicating for Cabot. The man thrashed wildly, trying to claw at Cabot's face. He could smell the whiskey on the man's breath. Cabot laughed in his face as he died. When it was over he left the body lying in the shadows, the man's money still tucked into his billfold. Cabot had plenty of money.

The plan that had formulated in his mind regarding Chance Sonnet stirred something dark and evil within his soul. This would be a special death; an exquisite death. He would reign over Chance Sonnet like a king.

Roaming through the sprawling ranch, he idled into the big kitchen where Maria, the new cook and housekeeper, was making bread. She had her hands in the dough and was kneading it gently. She looked up at him suspiciously when he entered the kitchen but didn't say anything. Cabot saw the alarm flash briefly in her eyes and this, too, gave him a sense of control over people. He enjoyed the fact that she was afraid of him. Cabot hadn't touched the woman — yet; but before long he would get to her, just as he got to all of the women who worked on his ranch.

He touched her shoulder and she flinched.

'Now don't you worry none, honey. I have a thought that you and I are gonna get along just fine.'

She ignored him, her face flushed a deep red, her hands trembling as she kneaded the dough. Laughing, he slapped her hard on the rump. 'You don't have any idea of what a fair and perfect gentleman I really am. Seriously, ma'am, I don't mean you any harm.'

She looked at him, perhaps because the sincerity in his tone belied his rudeness, and Cabot gave her all of his charming smile.

'Yes, señor,' she said quietly.

Come to think of it, he thought to himself, she isn't all that great, but I'll let her believe she is. In fact, he thought Maria was too heavy around the middle. He liked his women a lot younger. When they were young and supple they were also a lot easier to woo. A young girl fell for his charm a lot quicker than some middle-aged Mexican gal with a belly like a sack of potatoes. He winked at her and went from the kitchen.

Cabot was restless. He calculated the time it would take Lacey to ride out and fetch Halvar Borgstrom, the big Swede. Shouldn't be more than an hour, maybe an hour and a half. There was no getting around his anxiousness. He retrieved a bourbon bottle from his desk drawer and took it and a small glass with him out on to the porch. Sitting on a chair and watching the gate and the prairie beyond was manageable with the bourbon rolling over his tongue. With his insides warmed up he felt comfortable, and in charge again.

Thirty minutes later he saw dust on the prairie, and then two riders coming up fast. Lacey and Halvar rode on to the ranch and pulled up to the hitching rail. They dismounted and tethered their horses. Cabot admired Halvar's frame: six feet and with arms like ham hocks, a strong chin punctuated by blond hair that needed cutting. Cabot reckoned that Halvar was about thirty-five.

'Hello Halvar, come in and have a drink.'

The big Swede followed Cabot into the ranch house and took his glass of bourbon without speaking. He sipped it slowly, never taking his piercing blue eyes from Cabot.

'I want you to do something for me, and don't worry, you won't have to use a gun.'

'*Yah*, that's good. What is it that you want?'

Cabot told him, and the big Swede smiled.

8

In the morning the prairie was bathed in a golden light; the air was fresh and the pungent evergreens and pine trees bristled with small birds whose songs drifted to them on the morning breeze. The trees were laden with sunlight; the rolling plains alive with wildflowers and tall, swaying grass. For Jenny this appeared as no less than a paradise made all the more intriguing by the presence of Chance Sonnet.

Sonnet made a breakfast of bacon and biscuits, and Jenny helped make the coffee.

'You even have some sugar,' she remarked. 'It appears that you've thought of everything.'

'Let's hope so, but I guess I didn't think about meeting up with you and Toby here like this.'

Jenny looked around. 'This is a nice

100

camp, but we can't stay here for ever. What are you planning to do now?'

'I'm still thinking on that.'

'How long will you think on it? Today is a beautiful day, but this is Kansas, and it's tornado season.'

'You're persistent, I'll give you that. Like I said, I'm thinking on it.'

'What I know about Eric Cabot indicates he won't sit still.'

Toby, having finished his coffee, stood up. 'Mr Sonnet is fast with a gun. I'd say he's the fastest gun alive.'

'A gun is a tool like a saw and a hammer. Other men are just as fast.'

'But you're not afraid of Cabot. You're not afraid of anybody,' Toby said.

'Look, kid, what I did to you is nothing to be proud of. Being fast with a gun doesn't make a man special.'

'I had it coming. I never should have signed up for that fool job.'

'Let's just get you healed up and forget it. We'll rest up here a day and then I'll take you both to town,

101

somewhere away from Cabot and my problems.'

'Don't we have a say in it?' Jenny asked.

'No, I expect not.'

Sonnet couldn't but help to notice that Jenny's cheeks flushed red when she was angry, and the effect on him was startling. The brightness in her eyes, and the color of her smooth skin, and even the way the morning sunlight tangled in her hair left him feeling smitten. Sonnet was no fool. He could fall for this girl, and this wasn't the time for romance. He had to get her to safety as quickly as possible.

Before he could say anything further she stood up and announced, 'I need to clean up. It was a long ride and I'm filthy. While you're deciding our future I'm going to bathe in that creek on the other side of those trees. You just sit and think on things for a bit.'

She fetched her valise from the buckboard and strode off, the sarcasm in her voice hanging in the air like a palpable presence.

'She sure is something,' Toby said.

'Keep your nose in the books, kid.'

Toby laughed. 'I've been around saloons. I know what it's all about.'

'That girl is a different breed all together. I reckon she's like a wild horse.'

'I don't think she'd appreciate that comparison.'

'Aw, hell! Help me scrub out these tin plates.'

A short time later they could hear Jenny splashing about in the stream, and Sonnet noted with amusement that Toby kept turning his head in that direction even though the view was blocked by a thick line of trees and scrub-brush. He was relieved when she finally returned to camp. She had changed into a clean pair of brown slacks and a simple button-down shirt, none of which really hid her sumptuous figure. Sonnet had to stop himself from grinning at her when she came walking out of the trees.

'She sure is pretty,' Toby said.

'You two act as if you've never seen a clean woman before,' Jenny said as she noticed them staring at her. Sonnet couldn't think of an appropriate response, so instead he said, 'Let's fish that creek today and get ourselves a nice dinner.'

By noon they had four big catfish and Toby helped Sonnet clean them. Later, with Toby curled up under a tree once again with *Oliver Twist*, Sonnet decided it was a good time to survey the area, do some thinking, and get out of Jenny's direct line of sight.

'I'm going to look around a bit,' he said. 'You stay here with Toby. There's more books in my saddle-bag.'

'Don't you want any company?'

'No, you just stay here,' he said rather roughly.

He took his Winchester, went back to the creek, crossed it at a shallow point where some boulders helped him cross, and ascended a hill so he could look out in the direction of Dodge City.

They were in an area of gently rolling hills, very different from some of the typical flat Kansas plain. There was nothing but blue sky, swaying trees and birdsong on the wind. The day could not have been more tranquil. He took a breath and relaxed a little.

Sonnet allowed himself the luxury of relaxing only on rare occasions, and no sooner had he taken a breath and begun to let his mind wander when he noticed dust in the distance. A rider. He estimated the rider was a mile out. Further away, and off to the west, he saw more dust. Two other riders, following.

The riders could mean nothing, or everything.

He went and told Jenny and Toby about the riders.

'Do you think they're Cabot's men?' Jenny asked.

'Could be anyone. I want you and Toby to stay here near the buckboard. If they ride in and trouble starts use the buckboard as cover.'

They had not long to wait, but only one rider approached their camp. There was no sign of the other riders who, Sonnet knew, had been following the tall man who rode an old paint to the periphery of their camp. Sonnet stepped away from the camp a few feet, his Winchester held leisurely in his right hand.

'Good afternoon,' Sonnet said pleasantly.

The man grinned at him, his blond hair shining in the sun. '*Yah*, it's a good morning. And are you Sonnet?'

'I am.'

'I am Halvar Borgstrom. You heard of me, *yah*?'

'That I have. You fought twelve rounds on the Boston docks against Gordy Seldon. I heard you two fought to a standstill and neither man relented.'

'*Yah*, good.' Borgstrom smiled again; his smile was good-natured and infectious. Sonnet nearly smiled back. 'Now Halvar will fight you. If I win, Mr

Cabot pays me three thousand in gold and silver. This is good, *yah*?'

'That's good, but we won't fight.'

Borgstrom shook his head sadly. 'We will fight.' Slowly, he began climbing from his saddle.

Sonnet had his Winchester up quickly and jacked a round into the breech. 'No, we won't.'

Borgstrom stopped, one foot still in a stirrup. After a full minute of staring at Sonnet, he disengaged from the stirrup and held his arms wide. 'No guns, see?'

Sonnet shook his head, and kept his rifle pointed at the big Swede.

'If I go, men with guns will come back.' Borgstrom gestured at Jenny and Toby behind Sonnet. 'They will be killed. Is she your wife? How many guns can you stop? If we fight, you go free. You won't shoot. I am unarmed.' That grin again, wide and friendly.

'No, she's not my wife. What does fighting accomplish? If I win then Cabot's men will come anyway.'

'I want three thousand in gold and

silver. That's why we fight, and you won't shoot.' The Swede took a step forward.

Sonnet hesitated and glanced around. He had seen dust from several riders but there was no sign of them. Borgstrom was alone, but for how long? Sonnet's instincts were screaming at him to shoot the man, but he had never before shot an unarmed man. He couldn't risk wounding him. Even a bullet to the leg could prove fatal if it hit an artery.

The Swede threw a punch with his right hand. He was grinning as he threw it. Sonnet had no difficulty avoiding the punch. The Swede knew this and had thrown the punch simply to start the dance. Sonnet dodged, stepped back and said 'Hold on.' He set his rifle up against a tree, then he stepped forward. The Swede was big, but so was Sonnet, and he thought they were evenly matched. He would have to beat the Swede quickly.

'The gun.' Borgstrom said, indicating

the Colt around Sonnet's hip, 'We are men of honor, *yah*?'

Sonnet unbuckled his gunbelt and dropped it near his rifle. The Swede was smiling so widely his teeth gleamed like ivory and his blue eyes flashed with merriment. Borgstrom threw another right fist at Sonnet's head. This time the fist came in fast and with the Swede's shoulder behind it. The fist clipped Sonnet along his right cheek, and then Sonnet knew it was a knock-down fight. He had just avoided the full impact and his face stung from the blow. He reminded himself this was the man who had fought heavyweight contenders on the Boston docks.

Sonnet slammed a right into the Swede's ribs and he saw pain lance those blue eyes. Sonnet followed with a quick left and rattled the Swede's teeth. Now Borgstrom knew that Sonnet could fight, and Sonnet could hurt him. The merriment was gone from those blue eyes.

The Swede jumped forwards with

the quickness of a cougar, his fists cutting the air and connecting with Sonnet's chest and ribs. The two men circled each other warily. For ten minutes they circled each other and exchanged blows. Their knuckles were soon scraped and bleeding. The Swede had a split lip, the blood dribbling down his chin. This time when he tried to grin his teeth were flecked with blood.

'*Yah*, this is good. We fight like men should.'

'Too bad about the three thousand,' Sonnet said.

'I still win. You'll see.'

'Sure.'

So they continued, each man taking solid hits to the body. Sonnet felt that he could wear the Swede down, although it was going to take much longer than he preferred. The Swede connected with a flurry; a right cross that cut a gash across Sonnet's eyebrow and a short upper-cut to the sternum. Reeling backwards, Sonnet rammed his fist at Borgstrom's nose just as the big Swede was moving in for the knock-out punch. The nose didn't shatter, but it cracked, and tears welled up in Borgstrom's eyes as he grunted in pain. That split-second hesitation gave Sonnet the opening he needed. He landed a hay-maker on the Swede's jaw that snapped his head back and crossed his eyes. Without thinking, Sonnet tore into the man, landing his own flurry of punches on the Swede's head. He finished him with a hard uppercut that tore the wind from the Swede's lungs and put him on his knees.

The Swede squinted at Sonnet through the blood and tears. It seemed as if he were about to say something when Sonnet heard the *click-clack* of a Winchester being levered behind him.

'I reckon that'll do it, Swede; we'll take him now.'

Sonnet was diving for his rifle when a slug ripped up the earth in front of him. He cursed. Two men had come up behind them. One man had Jenny and

Toby at gunpoint, and the other had his Winchester pointed at Sonnet's head. Exhausted from the fight, Sonnet could do no more than look at the man in disgust.

'No!' Borgstrom screamed. 'We fight fair! This is not over!'

'Ease up, Swede,' the man said. 'You'll get the money. Mr Cabot said not to take any chances, is all. You was gettin' hit pretty hard.'

'*Yah*, the fight was not over,' Borgstrom said. 'I beat this man soon. You should not stop the fight.'

'Hell, Swede, you can drown your sorrow in beer and a pretty girl's arms.'

The man closest to Jenny shouted, 'Let's get on with it.'

'All right, Sonnet, turn around and get on your knees. Swede, you tie his hands.'

The man tossed Borgstrom some rope as Sonnet did as he was told, cursing himself silently. He should have shot the Swede. On his knees with his back to hired killers was the end of it

112

all, and he knew it. He felt bad for Jenny and the boy. They shouldn't have to see this. He glanced back at Jenny who stood by the buckboard with Toby. Her face was white and tears rolled down her cheeks. He looked away.

The Swede had tied his hands at the wrist. The rope was tight and cut into his flesh. He heard one of the men say, 'Deke, help the Swede get the coffin out.' He heard them pull the guns out of the coffin, and pull the coffin down into the grass.

'This is a real haul. Look at all of these guns.'

'We can sell that leather, too.'

The Swede grunted. Sonnet looked over his shoulder again. The Swede was carrying the coffin away from their campsite and out on to the prairie. Sweat ran down the Swede's face. Sonnet knew the coffin wasn't all that heavy, but the Swede had just taken a pummeling. Sonnet knew he had failed, and he knew he had built that coffin for himself. Cabot had won. Despair washed over him. He was going to die, but maybe that was for the best. Maybe, if he was lucky, he would see his wife and son again in heaven, just as the Bible said.

The Swede set the coffin down in the wind-touched prairie grass. One of the men followed him, raised his rifle, and fired three shots through the pine cover.

'That'll give him air until the boss gets here.'

The Swede lifted the coffin cover, examined the three holes, and dropped it on the ground. He walked over to Sonnet.

'You fight good.' Borgstrom said.

'Listen, that girl and boy had nothing to do with this. You let them go.'

'*Yah*, we see, maybe. Now you close your eyes.'

'No, you listen to me . . . '

Borgstrom struck Sonnet across the head with a powerful right. Stars exploded behind his eyelids. Another fist knocked the air from his lungs.

Sonnet was gasping for air as Borgstrom lifted him, half dragging him to the coffin. Sonnet tried to break free, lashing out with his arms hogtied. Borgstrom slammed a fist into his jaw. Sonnet barely felt himself being lifted and set inside the coffin. The lid was quickly placed on top and the sunlight vanished but for the three shafts of light that poured through the bullet holes. He gasped for air, his pulse pounding in his temples.

A shadow fell across the coffin and one of the men spoke: 'You listen, cowboy. You got air and you ain't gonna die. Leastways not yet. Now Bob here is gonna ride to tell Mr Cabot that we got you. That'll take till dark, so we won't see him till maybe noon tomorrow, or later. The Swede and I is gonna keep an eye on things. I'll shoot you if you try to get out of that coffin. Hell, just get used to it. We're gonna bury you in it tomorrow anyway.'

Sonnet twisted his wrists, testing the rope. His hands were firmly tied.

Damn! He hadn't planned it this way at all. He was going to die because of his own carelessness, and he couldn't stand the idea of what might happen to Jenny and Toby. But then he realized that Cabot's men had made one small mistake themselves. They hadn't killed him outright. His breath stirred the dust motes swirling in the shafts of sunlight that poured through the holes in the coffin lid.

Every breath he took in that pine coffin was a litany of vengeance.

9

Jenny watched in horror as Sonnet was dragged across the field and left in the coffin. She had never before felt so helpless. It was this feeling of helplessness, and the intrusion of these belligerent men, that filled her with outrage. They treated her as if she were stupid, confident in their actions, an unrepentant violence visible in their demeanor. She despised them.

'Don't you move, bitch!' the man had said, pointing his gun at her. His eyes swept over her figure and she could read his thoughts. The tone of his voice was grating. The man was pudgy, ugly, his eyebrows like dark caterpillars wriggling above his bloodshot eyes. The gray stubble of his beard contrasted with the yellow pallor of his skin. She resisted the impulse to lash out, to scratch his eyes out.

After the man they called Bob rode out of camp, the Swede and Deke rummaged through their belongings. They helped themselves to some jerky, and told Jenny to make fresh coffee. Toby stood near her as she made the coffee and she saw the anger etched on his features.

'We've got to stop them somehow. If I can get my hands on one of those guns Chance had in the buckboard . . . '

'No! Stop thinking like that. You can't shoot with that hand.'

Toby's face reddened.

'I'm sorry.' she said hastily, 'but we have to be careful.'

Then she remembered the derringer she had stowed in her valise. It was loaded with two bullets and she knew how to use it. But Jenny had never pointed a gun at another human being. The very idea filled her with dread. Deke had only glanced into her valise, grinning lasciviously at her undergarments and socks. The Swede had told him to leave those things alone, and he'd tossed the valise at Jenny's feet with a greasy smile on his sunburnt lips. The derringer was stuffed down into the valise, lost in the rumpled clothing.

The Swede and Deke drank their coffee and ate more of their food. Then Deke stretched out under a tree after telling the Swede to keep an eye on things. The Swede smiled glumly but said nothing. Jenny sensed that he was unhappy.

'What do you plan on doing with us?' she asked.

The Swede studied her a moment. His blue eyes were remarkably clear, and his long golden hair shimmered in the sun. But there were crow's feet at the corners of his eyes, and a sense of sadness emanated from him. Finally he said, 'Mr Cabot will decide. That is not for me to say.'

She looked out at the prairie where the coffin rested in the tall, swaying grass.

'What about him? He beat you fair

and square. You owe him something.'

The Swede's eyes flashed. '*Yah*, I owe him something. What do you owe him, woman? Why are you here?'

'I work for a newspaper, the *Nebraskan Weekly*.'

The Swede laughed and she hated him for it. 'You? A woman! I have time for only one thing with a woman, *yah*!' His laughter rattled her.

She was grateful when Deke fell asleep and the Swede spent his time idly watching the coffin as he whittled a sapling bough with a Bowie knife.

As the afternoon waned the windblown grass whispered in the sunlight. Over time, the coffin seemed as much a part of the prairie as the oak tees and wildflowers. It was like some permanent fixture, immobile and stoic, a reminder of mankind's mortality, a man-made monument to life's impermanence.

There was no sound from the coffin. Once, as the clouds drifted high above on the summer wind, a shadow fell across the coffin; but soon the shadow slid away as the clouds passed on, and the coffin was a part of the earth, the grass and the endless sky.

A cardinal landed on the coffin and made a song. It happened so swiftly that Jenny almost missed it, but there it was, and even the Swede saw the bird.

He looked at her and grinned. 'A red bird, *yah*! You saw it?'

'I saw it.'

The bird's song lingered a moment on the air, and then the rippling grass once again took up its task of whispering.

Jenny spoke with Toby briefly, asking him to sit tight with a book. As the idea blossomed in her mind, she wanted Toby to give the appearance of being submissive. Deke was snoring loudly. The man stank to high heaven and looked to be in poor health. That could work to her advantage if she could get Sonnet free of the coffin.

She thought about the derringer.

The Swede was idly whittling and keeping an eye on the coffin when

Jenny moved over to the buckboard and reached for her valise. The Swede saw her and asked, 'What are you doing?' He had stopped whittling and was eying her intently.

'I need some pills,' she said. 'I have indigestion.'

Rummaging in the valise, she touched the derringer, palmed it, and pulled out a scarf. 'I guess I left the pills at home. Sometimes I get a sour stomach if I drink too much coffee.'

'Then don't drink coffee,' the Swede said, and he returned to his whittling.

With the Swede's back to her she quickly stooped low and slipped the derringer into her boot. She folded up the scarf carefully and returned it to the valise just as Borgstrom glanced over at her again.

'Come away from the wagon. I don't want you near those guns.'

'I've never fired a gun in my life,' she said.

'*Yah*, good. Go sit by the boy.'

'I'm old enough to drink whiskey,' Toby said indignantly. 'I'm not a boy.'

Borgstrom shook his head in disgust and made no other reply.

Perhaps it was the stress of being held captive combined with the general excitement of her adventure that suddenly caused Jenny to take a long breath and stare wide-eyed at the world she occupied. With her heart beating madly in her bosom, it was as if the world had suddenly slowed down, and she moved as if wading through molasses. There was Toby sitting under a tree and reading a book by Charles Dickens; and there was Deke snoring loudly beneath another tree; and there was the Swede whittling absent-mindedly on a branch while keeping one eye pinned on the pine coffin. That coffin, which held the injured Chance Sonnet, was a grim reminder of the future. The coffin's existence was at odds, however, with the ripeness and the splendor of a warm summer's day.

She noticed a dark spot on the horizon. A purple cloud had edged into view from beyond the world's rim. The purple cloud was but a fragment, but still an intrusion. It irritated her the way a dust mote sometimes latches on to an eye and causes one to blink in frustration. A shock ran through her. Another storm was coming. They had barely survived a tornado and now, on this most beautiful and yet frightening day, yet another level of danger was being added to their predicament.

Jenny couldn't stand it. She had to resist the urge to pull the derringer from her boot and try shooting the Swede. Her lips trembled and tears sprang to her eyes. Toby saw her and started to rise, but she gestured for him to remain where he was. Despair cut at her like a knife.

They hadn't much time. In just a few minutes the purple cloud had grown on the horizon. Still, she was the only one who had noticed it. She smelled rain on the air. A bird whistled in a tree. The wind caressed the tall grass and the golden sunlight slanted down on the coffin. The sky slowly began to change from blue to green.

Borgstrom turned his head to the left and studied the horizon. He was on his feet, the Bowie knife and branch dropped and forgotten. He strode up to Deke and kicked him harshly in the shins.

'Get up! Look!'

A mountain of boiling clouds had reached up from the edge of the world and begun tumbling rapidly in their direction. Deke cursed, sputtered, and clambered to his feet. A sheet of rain was visible in the distance; it moved like a living thing and tore at the prairie. Half the sky was covered by rain clouds. It was as if they existed at the center point of two worlds, one of sunlight and warmth, and the other of raging winds and terrific storms.

Toby was on his feet and standing next to Jenny. 'What are we going to do?'

Deke heard him and glared derisively at him. 'I'm gonna tie that boy up. Can't have him runnin' off.'

'Tie him to the wagon,' the Swede said, 'and the woman, too.'

'You can't tie us up and leave us here!' Jenny nearly screamed. 'That looks like another tornado could strike. We need to move away from the storm!'

'You shut-up!' Deke took some rope and tied Toby to the buckboard wheel. He went after Jenny, and she impulsively scratched at him. He slapped her hard across the mouth and split her lip. They struggled briefly, but Deke pinned her arms at her side and pressed against her. His breath stank of tobacco. He lashed a rope around her wrists and tied her to a wheel as well, his hands touching her body as she slid to the ground.

'You and I is gonna have some fun later. You'll see!'

They watched the horizon. Before long the air was still and the rain came in torrents. When the rain eased off the air smelled of fresh grass and wild clover, but the birds had gone silent. The eerie silence added to the tension. Borgstrom saw the funnel cloud first.

'It comes near us.'

'Too damn close!' Deke cursed.

'Cut them loose. They can make it on their own. We have to watch him.' Borgstrom waved his hand at the coffin. Deke untied Jenny and Toby not thirty minutes after first tying them up. Jenny rubbed her wrists.

'You two won't get far, so I'll see you later.' Deke stared openly at Jenny's body.

'We're not going anywhere. You can't leave Chance in that coffin. He'll be killed if that tornado comes close.'

'It will come very close,' the Swede said. 'You are a fool. You love him, *yah*?'

'You said yourself that you owe him something. What kind of man are you?' Jenny was nearly sneering at Borgstrom. She spat at his feet. 'You're a man without honor!'

The Swede's face flushed red but he

didn't say anything.

'That tornado is comin' this way,' Deke said.

They all watched the spiraling mass of dirt and wind slither across the prairie; the sound of the wind had reached an unearthly tone. It sounded like the bleating of a thousand wounded animals.

Jenny felt a surge of panic. Reaching down into her boot, she pulled out the derringer, cocked the hammer and pointed the gun at Deke. When they heard the hammer click into place, the Swede and Deke turned and stared at Jenny.

'You let him out of that coffin!'

Deke said, 'Her hand is shaking.'

The Swede studied her with squinted eyes, chewing at his lip.

'You love him, *yah*. I understand.'

'We don't have time for this, Swede. That storm is comin' this way real fast. I can take care of this woman right quick.'

Deke rushed at her and pulled his

gun much faster than Jenny thought was possible. He was almost on top of her when she screamed and pulled the trigger.

10

Chance Sonnet watched the sky through the bullet holes in the coffin's lid. They hadn't nailed the lid into place. Knowing that he could easily push free only added to his problem because there was nowhere to go. The Swede or one of the other men would shoot him down the moment he was visible. He'd had a glimpse of the distance between the coffin and the camp before they pushed him into the coffin. There was no cover. There was no way he could traverse that distance, disarm one of the men, and then fight his way free. He went over it again and again, his mind in turmoil.

When a shadow fell across the coffin a shiver went down his spine. Once he heard the fluttering of wings followed by a bird's song. Time and time again he tested the ropes that bound his wrists but they had tied him without mercy. The ropes had chafed his flesh and his wrists were bleeding. He was exhausted, but that exhaustion dissipated immediately as he heard Jenny's scream followed by a gunshot.

He bent his knees, pushed up, rolled half out of the coffin, slanting himself towards camp so that he might spring to his feet and cover the distance as quickly as possible. He thudded to the ground. Seconds had passed and they all had their backs to him. He couldn't believe his luck. As he ran he was conscious of the green sky and the sound of wind behind him. The pungent scent of the earth and foliage hung in the air. He knew without turning to look that Kansas had intervened by some providential hand and sent another tornado slithering across the plains.

Jenny's shot had made a crevice in Deke's side, but the flesh wound wouldn't stop him for long. He appeared mesmerized by the sight of his own blood as he bellowed, 'She shot me! That bitch shot me!'

Sonnet brought both fists up and slammed them hard into Borgstrom's head. The big Swede grunted and tumbled as Sonnet yelled, 'Jenny! Shoot him!' Jenny raised her hand and aimed the derringer at Deke. Sonnet, taking no chances, kicked the Swede in the head. His boot made a sickening sound as it struck the man's skull and Sonnet wondered if he had killed the Swede. Deke was coming to his senses, his own gun hand rising, the muzzle pointing in Jenny's direction.

Sonnet couldn't make up the distance fast enough. It was then that Toby, still standing near the buckboard, screamed 'Watch out!' The single act of screaming distracted the befuddled Deke once more, and he turned his attention on Toby. Jenny fired again. Her bullet missed, but Sonnet crashed into Deke like an angry bull.

Sonnet pounded Deke with both fists lashed together, brutally. Having fallen to the ground, Sonnet was on top of him and beating him as Deke attempted to swing his gun hand around. Sonnet knocked the gun away and continued pummeling Deke. His fists slammed on to the man's face like a hammer. Deke's nose shattered and he screamed. His lips were split open, his teeth knocked out. He gurgled and spat blood.

Sonnet, yanking a Bowie knife from Deke's belt, cut the rope around his wrists by twisting the knife. Jenny was screaming. Sonnet heard her above the constant roar of wind and that of his own fevered blood pounding in his temples. His hands were soaked with Deke's blood. The man was alive, but just barely. Deke's face was a grotesque mask of pulped flesh. He lay on his back, his eyes swollen shut, and coughed blood.

Sonnet cursed him. With his own breath coming in rasping gulps, he staggered to his feet. He stumbled, picked up Deke's gun, and turned again towards Deke.

'Damn you!' Sonnet hissed. He pulled the hammer back.

'Don't! Please don't!' Jenny's hand was on his arm.

It was her voice that caused him to hesitate, although he never took his eyes from Deke.

'This man will kill you without thinking. He's an abomination!' he hissed.

'Please, let's go away from here. Please!'

'They put me in a coffin. They would have killed you and Toby.'

'Chance, please. Look at the storm.'

Instead he turned and looked at Jenny. The wind blew her hair back and in the muted light of a storm he saw the brightness in her eyes and the softness of her lips. She is, he thought, quite beautiful; and her gentleness and concern were like a wave washing over him. All of the anger fled from his soul and he was filled with a sadness that was crippling. He put his hand on her arm and pulled her closer; then he kissed her but once, softly, and broke away swiftly. She did not resist and stared at him in wonderment.

He turned and looked at the tornado racing across the prairie. The thought crossed his mind that he'd had about enough of Kansas tornados, although this one had arrived at an opportune moment.

Strapping on his gunbelt, he instructed Jenny and Toby to load the buckboard as quickly as possible. There was still enough time, and a direct route away from the tornado's path would put them out of harm's way. The wind was roaring in their ears and suddenly they felt displaced air rushing over them, warm one second and cold the next. The tornado was frighteningly close and they had trouble keeping their balance. The horse neighed, reared and tried to break free. The other horses had already broken free of their loose tethers and were racing madly away from camp.

'I'll kill you.'

Deke was on his feet, a long dribble

of blood slung from his broken lips to his boots.

'I'll kill you.'

Jenny and Toby had climbed into the buckboard. Sonnet was holding the horse's muzzle and trying to soothe it. Deke had no gun, no weapon of any kind. He stood there like some battered beast and cursed Chance Sonnet. Borgstrom was on his knees and when Sonnet saw the big Swede move he was oddly pleased. Somehow he sensed that Borgstrom now meant him no harm. The dismal dregs of defeat were visible in his eyes.

'*Yah*, you'll kill him, sure.'

Borgstrom moved towards Deke. Sonnet climbed into the buckboard and snapped the reins. The wind rattled the buckboard and their horse was panicking. There was no time left to do anything except flee.

The Swede grabbed Deke and gripped his neck with his hands. Sonnet saw the odd light in Borgstrom's eyes and wondered if he had damaged his brain when he kicked him. The Swede strangled Deke. They struggled but momentarily, and then Deke's legs bent at the knees as Borgstrom shook him furiously. He shouted in Swedish with his hands still clamped around Deke's neck, then he violently tossed the body aside.

The buckboard was buffeted by wind and dirt as the tornado cut a crooked path in their direction. The Swede turned and stared up at the twisting mass of debris that swirled at him with the fury of an uncaged beast. The Swede held out his arms in a crucifixion pose, tossed back his head, and howled.

The Swede was lifted from the ground, arms outstretched. Sonnet could hear him screaming in Swedish, then he was twisted upside down and pulled into the tornado to vanish in the blink of an eye.

Years later the dime novelists would say that Halvar Borgstrom fought the tornado to a standstill just as he had fought Gordy Seldon to a standstill on the Boston docks all those years before. They would say that every time a tornado touched down in Kansas, which was often, the big Swede's voice could be heard bellowing in the wind with the pure joy of battle. They would go on and say he is there still, roaring with the thunder and spinning on the wind, a smile creased across his lips.

Sonnet urged his horse away from camp, and the panic-stricken horse obliged just as the tornado changed direction, missing them by a hundred feet. Several times Sonnet thought the buckboard would be upended. They traveled in a haphazard direction that Sonnet thought might be north-west, but it was soon obvious they had lost any real sense of direction. The cloud-laden sky made it impossible to get their bearings by the sun or stars. In fact, the darkness that descended upon them might have been as much from the heavy clouds as it was from the setting sun.

They were soaked from the rain and littered with dust and grime from the wind. Eventually, Sonnet pulled to a stop and the three of them looked at each other in astonishment. Toby began to weep. Jenny saw his tears well up and his lips trembling. When Sonnet looked at him the tears were rolling down his cheeks. Jenny reached over and held his good hand.

'Let's get our bearings,' Sonnet said. They climbed out of the buckboard and Sonnet went and stroked the horse's muzzle. The horse had calmed down a great deal, but Sonnet could tell that she was still spooked. He said, without looking at Jenny or Toby, 'We all had it bad. There's no shame in that. If we take care of each other there's always hope.'

'It's all right now, Toby,' Jenny said.

'I don't know what's wrong with me.' Toby was embarrassed, his face flushed. 'I don't even know what I'm crying about.'

Sonnet went up to Toby and put his

hand on his shoulder. 'I know what you mean. Sometimes when I was up at my carpenter shop and it got late, I'd watch the sun go down and then it would hit me. I don't know why, except maybe sometimes living is cruel. You don't have anything to be ashamed of.'

Jenny was watching Sonnet.

'Hell, I caused all of this grief,' Sonnet continued. 'I'd take it back if I could, but I made some choices and this is all the result of that. The burden is mine. I promise I'll get you two safely away. Come on now, let's figure out where we are.'

They soon realized they had completely turned around and were uncertain what direction to take. They traveled for another hour and when they crossed a jagged creek Sonnet thought they must be traveling north. Another hour and they came to some rolling mounds. Jenny said they must be in the Smoky Hill area, and soon thereafter they came to a flat plain where some pueblo ruins were visible in the dirt.

'This is El Quartelejo.' Jenny said, 'I remember reading a sad story about a Taos Indian who met his lover here, but a jealous chief sent the warrior away and the girl died of a broken heart. This place is haunted by her ghost.'

'I reckon we'd better move on past here, then. I've plenty of my own ghosts and I don't need any more.'

Soon they came to divergent paths and Sonnet recognized tracks that must surely once have been part of the Butterfield Overland dispatch trail, judging by the wagon tracks that had solidified in the hard Kansas earth. The sky had begun to clear as the afternoon waned. The western horizon was streaked with yellow at the earth's rim, but the bowl of sky above them was lavender, and darkening quickly.

They had arrived at a place called Monument Rocks. Standing over fifty feet tall, the yellow cliffs were home to thousands of swallows, their wings making a tremendous sound as flocks of the birds swooped about the craggy cliffs. Sonnet wanted to get around one of the cliffs, putting the cliff between them and any riders coming from the east. When they made camp the sun was but a molten sliver at the world's edge.

They made a fire from the scrub-brush and ate some jerky and biscuits, followed by coffee. None of them spoke, their exhaustion evident on their features. It wasn't long before Toby was sleeping soundly on a blanket beneath the buckboard. The horse was hobbled near by, and Jenny set a blanket near the fire and stared absently at the flames.

Sonnet cleaned his Colt. He ejected the spent brass from the cylinder and tore the gun apart, wiping out each section with an old bandanna. He reassembled the Colt and loaded five cartridges, finally easing the hammer down on to an empty cylinder for safety. He did the same for all of the six-shooters that he had accumulated, and then for each Winchester rifle. He had a fine arsenal, and all of the guns were in perfect working condition. The fact that he had traveled so far with the guns of men he had killed was something of a miracle, he decided, but he also wondered at the value of such possessions.

After giving up his life as a carpenter he had wrought death, and death followed him. Jenny's voice was a soothing salve. It drifted to him across the tops of the flames, and, looking up, he saw the warm shadows that framed her face in the flickering light.

'What happens next?' Her voice was remarkably free of stress.

'Tomorrow we'll know if they try to follow us. There are numerous places in the tall grass where the buckboard wheels will be easy to follow, but there was a lot of packed, rocky earth, too. We can't escape them if they decided to pursue us, that's why in the morning I want you and Toby to take the buckboard and go west. I want you to follow the Smoky Hill River to a settlement called Russell Springs.'

'And what about you? Do you plan on staying here and letting them kill you?'

'You have to accept the fact that I am reaping what I sow. I'm sorry.'

'No. I'll send Toby in the buckboard. I know how to use a gun. I'm staying with you.'

'That's foolish. Even if Cabot and his men don't follow me, and I think they will, I'll be on foot.'

'You can't make me go, and you have to accept that fact. Now I'm going to get some sleep because we will undoubtedly have a long day tomorrow.'

Sonnet was so startled by her words that he found himself unable to speak. He sat glumly watching the flames; the tall cliffs seemed like an ominous presence in the dark, towering above them like an invisible weight that might crush them at any moment.

11

Captain William Samuelson Walsh, formerly of the Texas Rangers, understood instinctively that mankind were part of the landscape they inhabited. A man could not escape the land and the best men loved the wild country. The point was made to him yet again one morning as he stirred his campfire to life in preparation for making some Arbuckle's coffee. Replacing the comfort of his leather chair at his Texas ranch with the cold hard earth, a saddle blanket, and the steady creak of saddle-leather and the rhythmic clopping of hoofs on faraway trails was having a stirring effect on him.

Kansas wasn't his preference, but he had come to this flat, blue and green vista looking for Chance Sonnet, and he accepted Kansas for what it was. The long trail had awakened in him some dormant memories, and he had been filled with a sense of peace at what he had accomplished as a lawman; but now that contentment was tinged by a longing to do more.

That night he had dreamed of San Antonio in the old days, when in the spring the desert flowers bloomed and the river's surface rippled with small fish. On those hot summer nights the shadowy ruins of the Alamo mission were a cool place to which lovers might sneak away and enjoy the rapture of solitude; while on the riverbank little Mexican boys fished for their supper. Back then he felt as if he could reach out and touch this country's distant past; it was something tangible lying in wait in the cool shadows, and the footprints of men like Sam Huston, Davy Crocket, and Jim Bowie were still fresh in the Texas soil. Captain Walsh had followed his own course in history, and the trail had been one of hard work, bloodshed, but ultimate satisfaction.

Retirement had been appropriate for the time; now the trail seemed fresh again, and all of those feelings were because of a man named Chance Sonnet. When he was young, Sonnet was on the edge between turning bad or doing something else. Walsh saw a lot of himself in the young man, and he thought now how difficult it must have been for Sonnet to stay on the right side of the law after he lost his family. But he had remained a lawful man, though perhaps just barely at times. That was to his credit.

He glanced up at the sky and marveled at how beautiful it was; the morning was tranquil and lush with warm breezes, birdsong in the trees and the prospect of finding Chance Sonnet. Along the way Walsh had learned that Eric Cabot liked to throw his father's money around. The men liked him well enough, but the saloon girls all despised him. There was something there, Walsh thought, something about Cabot and young girls that was worrisome. He sensed instinctively that this fact was somehow linked to Chance Sonnet's vow to put Eric Cabot in a coffin. The details he could only imagine.

He packed up and was on the trail again very early. He had stayed clear of the storm and the tornadoes by detouring south, which put him slightly off the trail. Picking up the trail again was easy because of the wheel tracks in the grass. The rain and wind had not obliterated everything.

He found the remains of Sonnet's camp, along with the coffin in the grass, just before noon. He let his horse nibble at the grass after he dismounted and held the reins while pondering on the strangeness of such a sight. There were three bullet holes in the coffin's lid, which was lying off to the side. There was no blood. There were signs of several horses, but no horses. The buckboard tracks cut a path north-west through the grass.

There was one body. An obese man

with his neck purpled where strong hands had squeezed the life from him. The man's eyes were partly open, and black flies dotted his yellow and bloated face. Captain Walsh decided not to bury him. Cabot and his men would come, that was certain. Let them do the burying.

Unsheathing his Bowie knife, he went to work cutting loose large clumps of underbrush, which he cinched together with a lariat. He mounted his horse and spurred her on to the rolling plain of grass, pulling the branches behind him. He criss-crossed over the visible wheel tracks for a good mile, then, swinging back and polluting the trail, he returned to the coffin lying in the sun.

He untied the branches, dragged them near the camp and piled them in various places as if they had been windblown. He had bought Sonnet some time, but not much. A skilled tracker would recognize the duplicity. Walsh didn't know if Cabot had any skilled trackers with him, but he guessed that he didn't. So he had some time.

Briefly, Walsh considered waiting for Cabot. He thought he might set him out in the wrong direction, but he decided against that ploy. Cabot was going to meet up with Sonnet one way or another.

He decided to ride a circle around the mile-long area that he had swept with the branches, hoping to pick up the trail further north-west. He took his time, intentionally circling his own tracks to further confuse Cabot and his men. His own trail would be a mess, although not impossible to follow.

When he came to a creek he spent over an hour looking for a place to cross. The rains had swollen the creeks and rivers and an unskilled rider would put himself in danger by crossing in any deep, turbulent section. When he did cross the creek the cold water covered his boots and he cursed as the water sloshed down into his socks. Crossing without incident, he rode downstream and encountered an older man fishing in the creek. The man had two catfish pulled on to the bank and a sapling fishing-pole dangling in the water under the shade of an elm tree.

'I thought I heard a rider,' the man said. 'Why don't you set awhile and help me fry the fish. Name's Chip McTavish. Got a small place about two miles south-west of here.'

'That's right friendly, Mr McTavish. I'm Sam Walsh, Texas Rangers, retired.' Walsh dismounted, unsaddled his horse, hobbled it so she could nibble at some prairie grass, and pulled his only spare socks from his saddle-bag. 'Got caught in a high part of this stream. What's the name of it, anyway?'

'Don't know if it has a proper name. Some folks call it Jagged Creek or Ladder Creek. She comes off the Smoky Hill River north of here. What brings a Texas Ranger up this far?'

'Looking for an old friend, Chance Sonnet. Have you seen anyone else out here?'

Walsh gave McTavish a good look. The man was obese, jocular and red-faced. He had some trouble moving around because of his weight, and although the man's eyes sparkled with merriment there was a lazy slant in his attitude that bothered Walsh. He seemed to put the least amount of effort that was necessary into any movement.

'Not this week,' McTavish said. 'Not even an Indian brave; they're all being rounded up on reservations. Saw a wolf pack about two weeks ago. David DeWitt, he's got a place with his missus a mile from my homestead, he stopped by a few days past and told me about Chance Sonnet. Says he's gonna kill Eric Cabot.'

'Word travels fast out here.'

'David heard it from Karl Holmberg who heard it in Dodge City. That's the most excitement we've had in these parts since Wyatt Earp and Bat Masterson joined the Dodge City Police Commission.'

'Well, I think I'm getting close. I think he went northwest in a buckboard.'

'That would be up around Apparition Mound and Monument Rocks. The Indians say the place is haunted. There isn't a damn thing up there this time of year except heat, sand and rocks. I guess a man could hide out somewhat, but that's not an ideal place for a showdown.'

'Not many places are,' Walsh said. He stretched out his wet socks in a patch of sunlight and helped McTavish clean the catfish. They sat watching the fish fry in the pan.

'Do you know Sonnet?' McTavish asked.

Walsh nodded. 'He was a lawman once, but that was a long time ago.'

'Cabot's not so fancy with the ladies, leastways that's what I heard. He must have done something mighty bad to bring a gunman like Sonnet out of the brush.'

'I guess I'll find out soon enough.'

Walsh looked around and nodded. 'Hell, this is a sight better than my old armchair any day.'

McTavish chuckled. 'There is something about movin' about and seeing the land that can lift a man's spirit.'

They ate the fish and Walsh thought it was the best meal he'd had in some time, even if it was plain. They finished up with coffee, and Walsh gave the old-timer some of his Arbuckle's since McTavish was getting low.

'A couple of hours of riding and you'll see those cliffs,' McTavish said. 'There's nothing taller in all of Kansas. The Good Lord put those cliffs in a hellhole corner so you best make sure you and your horse have water. The water ain't easy to find after you cross the Smoky Hill River.'

'Much obliged.'

McTavish waved and settled down for an afternoon nap as Walsh rode away. From Captain Walsh's perspective, Chip McTavish was another reminder not to let himself go soft. The old-timer had it made but, while fishing in a stream was a noble past-time, Walsh didn't want to let himself get so out of shape as McTavish had. There was a lot of country left to see, and a lot of badmen that needed hanging. Once this was over he'd be giving some thought to saddling up again, maybe not full-time, but to keep his hand in the game.

When he came to the Smoky Hill River he repeated his task of finding a safe place to cross. The river was wide and swollen from the rain. The continuous sound of water tumbling across the shallow land made a roaring sound that was at once impressive and daunting. He had a sense then that he was being followed, or perhaps Cabot's men were on his back-trail sooner than he had expected. Walsh never ignored his instincts. That undefined sense — or second sight — that some men possessed was as strong in Walsh as it was in Chance Sonnet. A gunman learned when to rely on his instincts or face the prospect of visiting Boot Hill.

There was no hurry now. He cantered up and down the riverbank with an eye on the trail. At some point, depending on their level of intelligence, they would probably cross at the same spot where Walsh had crossed. It was a rocky area, and a bend in the river east and west, had slowed the tumult.

It was a solid hour and thirty minutes before he caught the sound of their voices on the wind. Two riders were skirting the river and looking for a place to cross. Walsh was vaguely surprised. He had expected more men. Neither man matched the description he had of Eric Cabot. They looked like common saddle tramps, mid-thirties, worn out and unshaven, smelling like a bunkhouse and a saloon combined.

Walsh spurred his horse and moved up to the spot where he had come out of the water. The two men hadn't seen him at first, but when his horse nickered they looked across the river in surprise. Each man had a Colt on his hip and a Winchester rifle in his saddle-boot. Their Stetsons were as worn as their features. What surprised Walsh the most was the fact that neither man wore spurs on his boots. These were two down-on-their-luck drifters. Watching them from across this narrow stretch of river, Walsh had a sense of how things were about to play out.

Before they could speak Walsh hollered across at them: 'Do you men work for Eric Cabot?'

They glanced at each other in surprise, and one of the men said, 'What's it to you?'

'That's not very neighborly,' Walsh said, frowning. 'If I had wanted to speak with men dumb as mules I would have ridden into Dodge City and had a beer with your likes at the Longbranch saloon.'

Again the two men glanced at each other, but this time they remained silent.

'I'll make it plain,' Walsh continued, 'just in case you two fancy boys get any foolish ideas in your thick skulls. Do you men work for Eric Cabot? It's not a hard question.'

'You callin' us fancy boys?' one man asked.

'Jesus! Are you that stupid?' Walsh shook his head in disbelief.

'We ain't no fancy boys. I got a woman waitin' on me.'

'Me too,' the other man said.

Walsh gave it some time as the two men stared at him incredulously. 'I'll tell you what, I apologize for mentioning fancy boys. I won't mention sheep either, if that pleases you. Now, I want to do you a favor. I have a notion that you two fellows work for Eric Cabot, and I'll bet you're scouts out looking for Chance Sonnet. Now isn't that right?'

The one man, perhaps the dumber of the two, tried to stop himself from shaking his head affirmatively. Walsh smiled. 'So I reckon you need to know that I don't want you crossing this river. By the way, where is Eric Cabot now?'

'He's about four hours behind us. What do mean, you don't want us crossing this river?'

'That means, you mangy fool, that I'll shoot both of you if you try.'

'You gonna try to shoot us?'

The two men appeared to be genuinely astonished by this revelation.

'I might shoot you anyway, just on principle. You two are the dumbest hired mules I've seen in a long time. You're an insult to humanity.'

Walsh saw the indignation on their faces and knew what was coming next. The man on Walsh's left pulled his gun first. His shot was wide, as expected, and at the sound of gunfire a flock of small birds suddenly burst free of the trees and scrub-brush that lined the banks of the river. The sound startled both men and their horses, which instinctively led them to gallop into the river with their guns drawn. Walsh yanked his Colt free, aimed, and fired at the man on his left. His shot slammed into his side and twisted him from his saddle. His horse, rearing back, startled the other man's horse, which hesitated and attempted to turn back to the shore. The man still in his saddle fired another wild shot at Walsh. This time Walsh could hear the bullet whizzing dangerously close.

Walsh holstered his Colt and pulled back from the river. The wounded man was thrashing about in the water and cursing. Walsh dismounted behind some brush, tethered his horse and pulled out his Winchester.

'You crazy old coot! I'm gonna cut your liver out and watch the buzzards eat your hide!' shouted the wounded man as he tried to grab his panicking horse's reins.

Casting his glance downriver, Walsh knew he couldn't get off a clean shot because the horses were rearing and snorting in fear. He didn't want to kill or injure the horses, so instead he jacked a round into his Winchester and fired twice down at the water just to keep them confused.

The man still on horseback emptied his six-shooter at the shore, perhaps not even realizing that Walsh had slipped away under cover of the brush.

'Damn it, Harley, I got shot! Help me out of this damn river.'

Watching the two men struggling towards the shore, Walsh was satisfied that their attempt to cross the river was temporarily halted. The wounded man plopped on to the opposite shore, clutching his side and wailing like a stuck pig. Walsh wasn't certain, but he guessed that with some medical attention the man had a chance of surviving.

Retrieving his horse, he mounted up and cantered down to the shoreline to watch the two men fumbling about. The other man had dismounted and was trying to get the wounded man's shirt off.

'Why don't you boys ride out?' Walsh shouted across to them. 'If you get him to a doctor he might even live. There's no profit working for Cabot any longer.'

'I'm gonna gut you like a turkey and

161

hang your innards on a tree branch!'
screamed the wounded man.

'That's downright unfriendly,' Walsh
said.

The man called Harley was quickly
reloading his Colt, the ejected brass
tinkling off his boots as he thumbed
fresh cartridges into the cylinder. 'You
sit tight, old man! I'll be comin' over
shortly with Larry here and we're
gonna have ourselves a time skinnin'
you alive.'

'Well, I'll be,' Walsh said, mostly to
himself. 'Some mule must have given
birth to these two jackasses.'

He backed his horse up and slipped
out of view. Stupid men were often just
as dangerous as skilled gunmen, and he
couldn't take any chances, any more
than he could ruthlessly shoot them
down. This was a dance of death that
would be played out on the prairie,
under the hot sun, and undoubtedly
before another hour passed.

He found some thick trees and scrub
and tethered his horse, moving quickly

away and downriver again. He stayed close to the river where there was the most cover. Squinting upriver he saw Harley and Larry galloping across the river and hollering like madmen. Walsh lifted his Winchester and fired swiftly. The bullet clipped Harley in the shoulder, then both men were out of view. He could hear them cursing and scampering through the brush. It sounded to Walsh as if they were dismounting and splitting up.

Harley came lumbering out of the brush on foot, his eyes pinched shut in pain, blood blossoming on his shoulder. Walsh jacked a fresh round into the Winchester and fired at a distance of fifty feet. The slug tore a hole through Harley's ribcage, exited out of his back in a fountain of blood, and spun him around. He dropped to a sitting position and facing in the opposite direction. He still held his gun. Walsh saw his body quiver and relax, the gun dropping soundlessly to the ground. Slowly, Harley's body tilted to the side and lay crumpled in the grass.

There was a noticeable silence in the air after Harley had met his maker. The birds had vanished, and there was naught but the steady roar of the river tumbling ever onwards.

From his spot in the underbrush Walsh shouted in his gravelly voice, 'Harley's dead, so why don't you give this up? I'll see to it that you get a doctor, and if you die I'll make sure you get a proper burial.'

In response to this Larry, stumbling in a rage from his hiding-place, burst free of the foliage and fired at Walsh with his Colt. The bullet whipped up dirt on Walsh's right. Slamming another cartridge into the breech, Walsh triggered the Winchester again and shot Larry in the chest. Remarkably, the bullet didn't slow him down although Walsh knew it was a fatal shot.

Larry lurched forwards, falling to his knees twenty feet from Walsh. He had fired five rounds and was trying to steady his arm to shoot Walsh with his last bullet. Walsh shot him quickly in the heart and waited until the body had stopped twitching before standing up and emerging from the brush.

The entire encounter had taken twenty minutes.

'Damn stupid boys,' Walsh muttered.

He rounded up their horses, unsaddled them, and let them go free. Someone would pick them up eventually. He tossed the men's six-shooters and rifles into the river. Then he dragged the two bodies to the river at the point where they had crossed and laid them out side by side with their hands across their chests and their heads resting on their saddles. Cabot would have something to think about when he found them.

Squinting at the horizon, Walsh mounted his horse and started out along the trail again. It was time to talk with Chance Sonnet.

12

Eric Cabot had five of his best men with him. The foreman, Lacey, rode at his side. They were followed by Bob, who had come back with the news of Sonnet's capture, and Girard, Burnham and Crazy Charlie. It was early in the afternoon when they approached the camp, sensing immediately that something was wrong. They heard a loud buzzing sound. As they drew closer it was obvious the camp had been vacated. When they found Deke's body they realized the buzzing sound came from the hundreds of black flies that had landed on the body.

'Look around for the Swede,' Cabot hissed.

They found nothing but horse tracks and wheel tracks in the grass, and the pine coffin resting on a hill in the sun. Cabot studied the coffin for some time.

'There's no blood, but there's three bullet holes in it.'

'Looks like one of them twisters hit this area pretty hard,' Lacey offered.

'That might have killed them all, except Deke here looks like he was strangled.'

'The wagon tracks go off thataway. We follow that and we might find the Swede and Sonnet.'

'We shoot to kill,' Cabot said. 'This has gone on long enough. I am just going to start shooting the minute I find them.'

None of the men disagreed. A strong feeling of apprehension had set in. Knowing that Sonnet had been captured but now appeared to be free was alarming.

It took them the better part of two hours to make sense of the confusing mass of hoofprints, but eventually they blundered on to the wheel tracks again. Lacey, being the best tracker in the group, commented that it appeared the buckboard was being followed by a lone rider. Even more disturbing, Cabot's scouts, Larry and Harley, had yet to report back. There was nothing to do but press on.

When they arrived at Ladder Creek they were surprised to see an overweight man fishing along the bank. When the man saw them he heaved himself to his feet with a grunt and waved.

'Howdy boys, name's Chip McTavish. This here prairie is getting to be mighty crowded. You must be this Cabot fella I heard about.'

Cabot's face flushed red with anger. 'Who told you about me?' he barked.

'A Texas Ranger, that's who. He's tracking this Sonnet fella that you're all looking for. I can't say I've seen this many riders out here in some time.'

Cabot was stunned. 'You said a Texas Ranger? What Ranger was that?'

'Sam Walsh, retired, or so he said. Pleasant fella. He gave me some coffee.'

'How long ago was this?'

'He rode out this morning. You boys

want some coffee?'

'What direction did he go in?'

McTavish waved at the trail to the north-west. 'He rode off towards the Monument Rocks. That's a godforsaken place. I expect if you go there you'll find him and this Sonnet you're after.'

For a moment Cabot considered shooting the fat man, but he decided he was harmless. 'If anyone comes up after us you pretend you never saw us, you hear?'

'Sure, I got nothin' to say about any of this. I'm going back to my farm today anyway.'

They rode off, leaving McTavish with a sense that somehow he had dodged trouble and that his farm was a sight more peaceful than the Kansas plains.

Cabot's men were getting uneasy, and they were itching for a fight. Kansas offered mediocrity in long stretches of deer trails and cattle trails. Lacey finally broke the silence.

'That's worrisome news about the Texas Ranger.'

'We'll be close to those rocks about

sunset. The way I see it we'll hold back, and go in at night. Maybe we'll send Crazy Charlie to find their camp.'

'They'll be able to see a long way from those rocks. Even at night, with a clear sky a man with good eyes can see things.'

Cabot looked over his shoulder at Crazy Charlie. 'Hey, Charlie, are you afraid of Chance Sonnet?'

Charlie, hearing his name mentioned, spurred his horse up alongside Cabot and Lacey. Charlie was the only member of the group not wearing a Stetson. His bald head was brown from the sun. He wore a deerskin vest over his otherwise naked chest. His arms were like melons, corded with veins.

'I ain't afraid of nothing. You pay me good and money is all a man needs if he knows how to fight.'

Cabot offered a menacing smile. 'That's good. I want you to go in when it's dark. See what you can see.'

'I'll do that.'

By the time they reached the Smoky

Hill River the sun had dipped to the tree line and the light was fading fast. The trees threw long shadows across the prairie. There were plenty of horse tracks to follow and they found a shallow bend in the river to cross over. Coming up out of the cool green water they reined in their horses suddenly, staring in slack-jawed disbelief at the two bodies that had been displayed for their benefit.

'That's why Larry and Harley never came back,' Lacey said.

A black crow was perched on Harley's face. The bird had pecked the eyes out and now flapped its wings with irritation as the men dismounted and walked up to the bodies. The crow shrieked and flapped away.

'They've been shot,' Cabot said.

'That isn't right,' Girard said. 'Harley wasn't much at poker but he was a good cowpuncher.'

'Drag their bodies into the river,' Cabot ordered. 'They're starting to smell already.'

'We ain't gonna bury 'em?' Burnham asked.

'You heard me. Drag them into the river. We'll make camp here. Lacey, you and Charlie circle about a mile around to make sure we're not being ambushed here.'

Grumbling to themselves, Burnham and Girard dragged the bodies into the river. Lacey and Charlie went riding out to reconnoiter the area. Cabot then ordered Girard and Burnham to make a fire and get the coffee boiling.

When Lacey and Charlie returned they reported that the trail was easy to follow now and there was no sign of anyone waiting in ambush, at least not yet. When the coffee was ready they sat around the fire and Cabot set his gaze on Bob.

'Tell me about Sonnet. Everything you can remember. And then the woman and the boy.'

'Sure, boss. He was about six feet, tough as nails when he fought the Swede. He had the Swede beat, that's for sure.'

'How did the Swede take that? He doesn't lose often.'

'I dunno, the Swede is the Swede. Deke had his eye on that woman. She had a nice figure. You know the boy — Toby, that skinny kid in town; well, he was injured.'

'They didn't say where the woman came from?'

'No, only that she wasn't his wife. She reminded me of a schoolmarm, except prettier.'

'Did that kid Toby say what happened to him?'

'Not when I was there. I left right quick once the fight was over, just like you said to. I never heard anyone say he was traveling with a woman, and they never mentioned a Texas Ranger.'

'We don't know what we're up against,' Lacey said, 'Sonnet is a killer, but he can't take all of us. I say we go in at once and shoot them all. There's no better gunmen than Girard and Burnham here.'

Cabot nodded. 'I want to know

exactly where they are, so we'll stick with the plan. Charlie, you take Bob here tonight and pinpoint their position. Once we know where they are we can kill them.'

'Even the woman?' Lacey asked.

'Yeah, even the woman.'

Nightfall came swiftly and Charlie and Bob set out, with the sun just a sliver of gold on the horizon. They took their time moving across the dusty plains and before long they could make out the chalky shapes of the area called Monument Rocks in the light of a half moon. They stopped and dismounted. Charlie took his Winchester and told Bob to keep the horses hobbled while he went in for a closer look. Bob, not being either industrious or brave, was happy to comply.

The rocks were clustered by themselves on the plains — two sections and connected by an animal trail — a lonely and unusual sight amongst the grasslands and flat prairie that surrounded them. Crazy Charlie could look in any direction and see nothing but flatlands all the way to the horizon. He had ridden past this area once, years before, and he recalled there were many nooks and corners, arches and buttresses, where a man might hide. Yet the area was not all that large, and once a man was pinpointed he would be an easy target. There were scant places where a rifleman could climb to, and there was no cover. He decided to circle the rocks, keeping low.

Angling left, he stooped and began to circle from the western side. Once, he thought he heard voices and he stopped. The half moon was bathing the landscape in a silvery light, and the chalky rocks stood out in contrast to the lavender sky. He had already decided to kill anyone that he encountered. The boss wouldn't mind, of that he was certain. He would probably get a bonus of silver coins once he reported that they were all dead.

Taking a chance, he slipped up close to the rocks on the furthest north-west section by his estimation. Creeping to an edge, he peered around and finally saw the buckboard. The buckboard was pulled out of sight, standing near a taller section of rocks. In order to see it a man would have to circle inside. A good place to stay out of view from riders in the distance. A campfire near by had burned low but the embers were still glowing.

Crazy Charlie let his eyes roam among the rocks in every direction, looking for any movement. There were two people sleeping on blankets near the buckboard, but in the gloom he couldn't discern their features. He considered opening fire with his Winchester. That would take care of two of the four, but he didn't like the idea that there were two more men out here somewhere. The thought made perspiration break out on his forehead. Sonnet had killed everyone whom Cabot had sent after him, probably including, Crazy Charlie knew, the Swede. Crazy Charlie wanted to kill

Sonnet and the Ranger first, and then he would take care of the woman and the boy.

Something stirred in the darkness.

It was more of a feeling than a sound, really, and Crazy Charlie didn't like it. No, he didn't like it at all when the snakes began to writhe in his belly and his mind was clouded with anger; he didn't like it when that prickly sensation washed over his skin and he felt that he was being watched.

But there was nothing there, nothing at all.

There was the warm night wind, which brought with it the whispers of old Indian camps, the barely perceptible gossips of time that left their mark on the dry and forlorn plains. There were ghosts here, and someone else. Involuntarily, Crazy Charlie shivered, and then, without meaning to, he cursed.

'Damn it to hell!'

He hadn't quite shouted the words, but they had been flung from his lips before he could stop them. Sweat trickled down his forehead. He stopped, crouched, and waited. His pulse beat in his temples and his mouth was dry as bark. He looked behind him and there was nothing. He scrutinized the cliffs, thinking that somehow, impossibly, Sonnet had managed to climb straight up.

The wind greeted him with its caressing touch; far in the distance a wolf howled at the moon.

The silvery landscape was a place unreal; ancient and haunted, the land carved by wind and rain and the lost oceans of centuries past.

He clenched his teeth. His palm was wet with sweat as he gripped his Winchester. Minutes passed that seemed like an eternity. He didn't move. He didn't dare turn his head. Whatever had spooked him was near by. He could sense it, although he saw nothing. For a moment he feared that he had gone mad.

His heart sank when he heard the

voice. It was a calm voice, commanding, self-assured.

'Turn around slowly as you drop the rifle and stand up.'

The rifle slipped from his sweat-stained palm. The silhouette was six feet tall, the eyes blazing with an inner light. He knew who it was, and the man had bested him so easily, so damn easily.

Chance Sonnet swung his Winchester in a wide arc and with such terrific force that when the walnut stock slammed into Crazy Charlie's jaw the bone shattered and teeth spewed from between his lips with an eruption of blood.

13

The previous morning, dawn broke silently and the prairie came into view as the sun slid up from the purple horizon. Sonnet listened to the birdsong and kept an eye on the plains for any sign of riders. The night had been uneventful although Sonnet wasn't foolish enough to believe they would spend a second night here without encountering trouble. With Jenny and Toby still sleeping, and just as the birds began their morning chorus, he went about the business of placing his guns at various places among the rocks in preparation for the coming battle.

He paced off the distances and guessed how fast he would need to run before reaching one of the rifles. Satisfied, he returned to the camp to find Jenny making coffee.

'We have plenty of food,' she said,

glancing up at him. 'Maybe three days' worth. How long will we be here?'

'I was hoping you'd reconsider: take Toby and set out for Russell Springs.'

'It might be better if you let me use one of the rifles. I'm not so steady with a pistol.'

Sonnet grunted. She had made up her mind. Toby was watching him with curiosity.

'Kid, you have a chance to go, and you can take the money with you.'

'Aw, I ain't goin'. You know that.'

There was nothing more to say so they drank coffee and ate some biscuits. After breakfast Sonnet took them both around the rocks and cliffs and explained his plan. Neither Jenny nor Toby asked any questions, but they looked earnest enough. Sonnet knew he was their only chance.

That was what he thought, at least, until later in the afternoon when he spied dust in the distance. After some time he determined it was a solitary rider. There was no other movement on the plains. He waited patiently as the rider ambled into view. His instincts eventually told him this wasn't one of Cabot's men. As the man came closer he looked vaguely familiar. Recognition blossomed in him, but not until the man was forty feet away. Sonnet was astonished. It had been a very long time since he had last seen the tough-looking rider who cantered up to him. Sonnet had his Winchester across his arms as he leaned against the rocks.

'Howdy, Sam. I thought you was dead.'

'Damn near a few times.' Walsh looked down at his old friend, his eyes twinkling. 'I was sitting in my leather chair and reading a book when I got word you were gunning for Eric Cabot.'

'Is that right? All the way down in Texas? They use to say Texas was as far away as a young man's dream, but close enough for trouble.'

'I'd have to agree with that.'

'We have some coffee and biscuits.'

'I heard you was with a woman and a boy.'

Sonnet nodded. 'Come on down and meet them. There's going to be a sight of trouble coming in behind you.'

Walsh dismounted and led his horse by the reins. 'There's going to be two less. I met up with them at the Smoky Hill River. Cabot's about four hours behind me.'

'I've got plenty of ammunition.'

'We'll need it.'

Sonnet almost grinned at the word 'we', but he remained stoic with the exception of pausing a moment and looking Walsh in the eye. Then Sonnet gave a little salute off the brim of his Stetson with his fingertips, and Walsh nodded in return.

Jenny had a rifle in her hand when they turned the corner. Sonnet was impressed.

'I heard voices.' she said.

'This is Captain William Samuelson Walsh, but his friends call him Sam.'

Walsh tipped his hat to the lady and

nodded at Toby. 'I'm glad to meet all of you. I've had a long ride. Now how about that coffee and we can sit a spell and figure out what to do about the trouble that's coming.'

As they drank their coffee Walsh filled them in on his trip, ending by giving the details of his encounter with Cabot's men. When he was finished he listened as Toby told how he had been hired by Cabot and nearly killed, only to become friends with Sonnet. Jenny told her story, too, and finally Walsh asked the inevitable question. 'Why do you want Cabot dead?'

Sonnet said bluntly, 'He did wrong by a young girl in town where I lived. I guess she didn't know what else to do, so she hung herself.'

Walsh's surprise showed on his face. He whistled between his teeth and pushed back his Stetson from his forehead. 'That's it? Cabot didn't kill anyone himself? He got tangled up with a girl you knew?'

'He's got to be accountable.'

'You're going to murder him.'

'He's accountable.'

'Why is it your business? Why kill him over a girl that couldn't handle being jilted?'

'Because I can. Her name was Lauren. She was the same age as my son. I was a carpenter, went by the name of Frank Neal. She watched me work and told me about her dreams. After Cabot came and left, she was all busted up. When she died it brought back a lot of memories.'

Walsh cursed softly and shook his head. There was a long pause and none of them spoke. Walsh saw the tears in Jenny's eyes. She wiped away the tears. Sonnet hadn't seen it because he was staring at his coffee cup. Toby was stoic. Walsh was piecing things together in his mind. Eventually, he thought he had a clearer view of things than Sonnet. He felt so much sympathy for his friend. Sonnet had experienced many things in his life, but so much of it involved grief.

'I've got a spread near Dallas that I

lease out. A man named Paco runs it for me, but he's getting up in years. The spread is yours if you want it.'

'I hadn't thought about what's next.' Sonnet said.

'I know. Hell, Chance, you've been consistent in everything you've done all your life. You're always backing up those that need help. I don't have to tell you what's next. Look around.'

Sonnet glanced up at Jenny and Toby. 'I'll consider your offer, Cap'n. There's still the immediate problem of Cabot and his men.'

'That'll depend on a lot of things. How many men he brings being our primary concern.'

Sonnet told them how he had placed the guns around the rocks, and his plan to keep moving and to keep shooting.

'That's reasonable, and I don't think they know I'm here. We'll need to put Jenny and Toby here in a place that offers the most protection.'

'I've got that figured out,' Sonnet said.

The buckboard was pulled across the opening beneath an arch. With their backs to each other, Jenny and Toby could fire in each direction. Toby said he could balance a rifle on the buckboard with his bad hand and fire with the other. He wouldn't be aiming, but he could keep the lead flying. Sonnet and Walsh could move at will around the rocks and fire on any intruders.

'It might work,' Walsh said.

'It only takes one bullet to stop a man. I have some experience hitting my target.'

'That you do. Yep, it might work.'

'We'll make it work.'

Jenny, who had been silent this whole time, looked at Captain Walsh and said, 'Can't we all just ride away, now?'

'I'm afraid not. Cabot won't let this go. Now I'm not a judge, but technically Chance here hasn't broken any laws. All of the men he's killed have attacked him first. So when they come later today you'll have to sit tight and let them draw first.'

Sonnet and Walsh spent the afternoon walking the perimeter and keeping an eye on the trail for signs of dust. By late afternoon the wind had died down and an eerie silence descended on the plains. What small breeze they felt did no more than rustle the dirt with the same effect a butterfly's wing might have. There was a faint haze at the horizon, the remnants of all of the dust the storms had kicked up. The late afternoon sun filled the air with a golden sheen and out across the plains by the rivers and creeks the cottonwoods suddenly came alive with birdsong. Oddly, the many birds that nested high in Monument Rocks were silent. The distant sound of life along the trail was barely perceptible except to men like Sonnet and Walsh, whose keen perceptions had been honed by life on the wild western trails.

'I reckon they're waiting,' Walsh said. 'I might have spooked them, leaving those bodies for them to find.'

'They'll come tonight, try and sneak up on us.'

They decided to eat again, and Jenny made more biscuits with the flour. There was dried beef strips and bacon, too, which they ate greedily. Toby ate the most. After eating, Jenny checked Toby's wounded arm and remarked that it was healing up nicely. They would let the fire burn low and wait for nightfall.

When the sun set the sky turned into a conflagration of purple and orange, and the feeling of unease seemed to spread like the growing pools of lavender darkness. Jenny and Toby stationed themselves in the buckboard. There was no shortage of ammunition, and they could fire at will in two directions. Sonnet had given them firm instructions not to leave the buckboard unless he told them to. Walsh and Sonnet each had a Winchester rifle and a Peacemaker Colt.

Waiting was always the hard part. A

man waits for something when danger was near and his belly gets full of rattlesnakes.

The darkness was like a cloak that muffled all sound. Eventually, the half-moon arced in the sky and peered like a sentinel over Monument Rocks, offering them reasonable visibility. The world was bathed in a faint silvery glow and when they moved their shadows rippled over the crevices at their feet.

Sonnet thought he heard something straight out along the trail, and his instincts told him this was no illusion brought on by the sinister touch of night. The whinny of a horse sounded, unheard by all but them, far down the trail at that point where the rocks were visible as towers reaching for the stars. They were there. Cabot's men.

'Go back and tell Jenny and Toby to fix up those blankets like I said, so it looks like they're sleeping. I don't think it's but one or two yet, and I want to draw them in.'

Walsh slipped away.

Sonnet examined the cliff face and situated himself in a craggy line where the shadows were deep. He was standing in plain view but blending with the darkness. He was relying on being unseen by a gunman who would expect a trap, but not one in front of his eyes. A nervous man might walk past without noticing him. The night was alive with shadows and the texture of the cliffs and dim light worked to his advantage. Walsh, he knew, would find a similar place to wait: to wait and to watch.

He sensed the man before he saw him; and then a fleeting shadow caught his eye. The man was crouched low, running hard. He came up against the cliffs far down on Sonnet's right. He was surprised the man was alone, although it was obvious there were more men down the trail. He wondered how many.

Sonnet was patient. He dared not move. The man came up slowly and craned his neck around a corner. He had a view of the buckboard. The man hesitated. He had a rifle in his hand but he didn't raise it. Sonnet could smell the fear coming off the man; his fear was as pungent as sweat. The man was constantly whipping his head back and forth, but he was looking without seeing. He seemed to stare right at Sonnet, then in an instant he was looking elsewhere.

When the man moved away Sonnet followed him, slowly. They had reached a point where the man was going to make a decision, and he paused. Perhaps he sensed Sonnet coming up behind him. When the man turned around Sonnet hit him hard with the walnut stock of his Winchester; teeth and blood spewed across the rocks. The man went to his knees delirious with pain. He was groaning, semi-conscious, his eyes squeezed shut, the tears rolling down his cheeks and mingling with his bloody mouth.

Sonnet stripped the man of his rifle and gunbelt. A few minutes later he called out to Captain Walsh and together they went and looked down at the man with his jaw destroyed.

'Let's strip him down to his long johns,' Sonnet said.

The man was in no condition to protest. They yanked his boots off him, along with his vest, shirt and trousers, and left him barefoot and wearing his red long johns.

'Can you talk?' Sonnet asked. 'What's your name?'

The man lifted his head and stared in abject terror at his captors. He gurgled a response. 'Char . . . Charlie . . . '

'Anyone with you?'

Charlie nodded.

'Where?'

Charlie pointed out at the trail. 'Not . . . not . . . far.'

'How many men does Cabot have with him?'

Charlie held up five fingers.

'So he sent two men in tonight, is that right?'

Again Charlie nodded.

193

Sonnet looked at Walsh, then he studied Charlie for a long minute, his eyes grave. There was no sound but for the whimpering of Charlie; the blood on his face was congealing into a black mass.

'Wait here,' Sonnet said. 'I'll see if I can persuade his friend to join us.'

Moving warily along the trail, following a path of moonlight and guided by instinct, Sonnet went looking for the other man. It took him twenty minutes, but he found the man when a horse whinnied and the man said 'Hush, now.' Changing direction, Sonnet slipped over a rise and saw the man with two horses. They were just over a mile away from Monument Rocks.

He jacked a round into the Winchester and yelled 'Hold it!' as he raised his rifle. One of the horses spooked and broke free. The man cursed and flung himself into the other horse's saddle. Sonnet hesitated. If he fired he would hit the horse, which had reared on its hind legs and was spinning about. Spurring the horse, the man galloped away. Sonnet lowered the rifle and let him go. He wouldn't shoot a man in the back. Hell, he'd see him again soon enough anyway.

Trudging back to camp, he thought about the man named Charlie whom he had busted up. The man was a sniveling fool, but still dangerous. Back at camp, Walsh was leaning against the rocks and Jenny and Toby had come out to watch after Walsh had given the all clear.

'He got away,' Sonnet announced. 'I suppose that's for the best.'

'What will we do with this one?'

'He's going back to his friends.' Sonnet crouched down and looked into Charlie's eyes. 'You listen up. You can walk out of here. Tell Cabot I'm waiting on him, but if you come back with him then I'll shoot you. Do you understand me?'

Charlie nodded meekly.

'That's good. You tell Cabot he's riled up an army of ghosts and they're marching his way. You tell him.'

Sonnet's voice had gone flat and hard. Hearing him speak, Jenny felt a cold shiver run through her. At that moment the birds that rested high in the rocks fluttered to life and swooped into the night sky. The sound of their flapping wings was ominous and sounded to Jenny like a harbinger of death.

14

Crazy Charlie loped across the dusty trail with his feet bleeding from the sharp rocks that he stumbled over. He was pursued by shadows and his mind reeled with fear. Every dark corner, every windswept shadow held a thousand monsters. Drool flung from his busted lips as he took in a lungful of air, wheezing and coughing, lurching like a drunk along a crooked trail.

That man had humiliated him. That man that Mr Cabot wanted dead. And Charlie had failed; Charlie had lost his nerve.

Fear propelled him onwards; fear and, eventually, anger.

The pain was nearly unbearable. His jaw and head hurt so badly that he could barely keep his eyes open. The blood had congealed around his mouth and now a deep and abiding ache radiated throughout his skull.

He panicked when he discovered that Bob and the horses were gone. Had that man Sonnet killed him? He ran blindly into the night, short, plaintive cries of fear and pain bubbling up from his throat as he stumbled along. Eric Cabot was staring at him with open hostility when he came shambling into their camp.

'What the hell happened?' Cabot demanded. Bob was there with the horses, and Lacey, Girard and Burnham looked surprised to see him. Charlie pointed at his broken jaw.

'See what he did! The man ain't human!'

'Where are your clothes? You look like a damn fool.'

'We can kill him, boss! We just haveta take 'em slow like, kill 'em all one at a time?'

'He's not alone? How many men does he have with him?'

'I saw another man and that was all.'

'You crazy bastard! I should shoot

you myself right now.'

'We should send for more men,' Lacey suggested. 'Sonnet has killed or wounded everyone who's gone up against him so far.'

Cabot shook his head dismally. 'I don't want to wait this out. This has all gone on far too long as it is. I don't know this Sonnet at all, but I'm going to kill him.' He looked at Girard and Burnham, his two fastest gunmen. 'You worried, or will you take on Chance Sonnet right now?'

'It's not about being afraid,' Burnham said. 'I'm not afraid of dying, and I'm not afraid of Sonnet. You hired me because I'm fast with a gun.'

'Same here,' Girard said. 'It's about the money.'

'All right,' Cabot acknowledged. 'I'll give you both a thousand-dollar bonus in gold, no matter which of you kills him. Just get it done.'

'That's in addition to our regular pay?' Girard asked.

'Yeah. On top of your pay you each

get a thousand dollars in gold.'

'Then let's kill them before sunup,' Burnham said.

Cabot told Charlie to follow on his horse and to use the rifle Lacey gave him. Charlie, too frightened to resist, and still somehow harboring the desire to redeem himself, climbed into the saddle. The stirrups hurt his swollen feet and he made a silent vow to kill the man who had discredited him and caused him such discomfiture.

They rode hard and fast, making no effort to conceal themselves any longer.

Propelled by greed, they spurred their horses mercilessly; the night's tranquility was shattered by the thundering hoofbeats of gunmen who refused to acknowledge fear.

When they saw the cliffs rising in the distance they spurred their horses yet again. Cabot screamed, 'Split up and circle the rocks. Shoot anything that moves.'

Cabot veered right with Lacey; Girard and Burnham spaced out and turned left, circling the long way round. Charlie, suddenly frozen with fear, galloped headlong into an opening that cut straight through the largest section of cliffs.

In his haste he let go his reins and his horse slowed to a canter. The silvery moonlight made the shadows deep and cast an eerie glow off the crevices and outcrops. A long shadow seemed to slither into life and he raised his rifle, levered a cartridge into the breech, and fired twice rapidly. The slugs tore up rock splinters and dust, whining off the stones, and ricocheted into the unknown.

Something moved to his left and he heard a man grunt. Twisting in his saddle, he jacked another round into the breech and fired at a shimmering spot in the darkness. He heard the shot slam harmlessly into stone.

'God damn you!' he yelled. 'My feet hurt! You see what you done to my feet? And I got teeth missin' here.'

His horse suddenly reared back and

tossed him from the saddle. He hit the ground so fast and so hard the wind was knocked from his lungs. Gasping for air, he clawed at the earth until his fingers found the rifle that he'd dropped as he fell. The good fortune of keeping his rifle seemed to revitalize him, and Charlie sucked in a lungful of dry air.

Bursts of gunfire rang out from two separate locations. Desperately, Charlie crawled to a wall, hunched low, staring about in terror. There were too many places for them to hide. The gunfire erupted again, echoing in the north and in the east. As the desperate shooting continued, he could hear Cabot's men shouting and snarling as they waged their attack. Then the shooting stopped just as suddenly as it had started. He thought he heard a horse whinny; and then, after several agonizing minutes, he heard horses galloping near by. But he saw nothing.

The night breeze picked up and nudged the dust. The moonlight cast a silvery sheen over the wind-blasted rocks and the shadows seemed to tremble. Creeping along the wall, he snapped his eyes back and forth, hoping to spot Sonnet. He wanted so badly to kill Sonnet. He wanted to put his hands around Sonnet's neck, to crush his windpipe with his thumbs, and to watch him slowly die. Then he wanted the woman. He wanted her all to himself, right there in the buckboard.

Charlie stopped suddenly. Something moved in the darkness and caught his eye. A man had come around the corner fifty yards away. The man had glanced in Charlie's direction, but then looked away. He hadn't seen Charlie slinking along the rocks. Charlie raised his rifle and planted the buckhorn sights on the shadowy figure. As his finger curled around the trigger the man quickly slipped back around the corner, almost as if he sensed the danger.

A burst of rifle fire rattled out: *Blam! Blam! Blam!* Then the night fell silent again. The shooting had been closer this time. Charlie felt sweat dripping off his bald head. He continued his slow progress along the cliffs. He sensed eyes watching him. His mouth was dry again. Once more the cold, reptilian fear came alive and uncoiled in his belly.

A volley of shots crashed across the dusty landscape and several bullets chipped away at the rocks over his head, showering him with dust and shale. He scampered away just as Burnham galloped into view, anger etched in his face, his Winchester leveled at Charlie.

'Don't shoot, Burnham! It's me, Charlie!'

Burnham reined his horse to a stop and looked down at Charlie with a combination of revulsion and anger. 'You damn crazy fool!'

'Where's the others? Did you kill Sonnet?'

Dark eyes squinted at Charlie. 'He's like a phantom. You stay here and shoot anything that's not on horseback. Sonnet's on foot, as best we can tell.'

Burnham spurred his horse and galloped out of view before Charlie could think of anything more to say. His stomach did flip-flops. Staying put was something he was convinced would get him killed. He had no intention of doing any such thing.

Yet another burst of rifle fire startled him into moving. The hammering echoes of Winchester rifles unleashed around the corner propelled Charlie into a leaping gait; his palm felt sweaty on his own rifle's lever. Then he remembered how to find the buckboard, which was now situated under an arch of rocks. He decided to swing around and come at it from the outside, sneaking up along the jagged cliff face.

The gunfire was still incessant, but it had moved away in a circling pattern. Charlie had a sense that Sonnet and Cabot were constantly moving, playing cat and mouse with each other, and that might offer him an opportunity to sneak up on the woman. The notion struck him that he might hold her hostage to draw Sonnet out, and he could use her supple body as a shield.

Grinning to himself, Charlie scooted along the wall, his feet throbbing with pain. When his aching feet stumbled into a pile of clothes he looked down with his jaw agape. His clothes and boots were still piled where Sonnet and Captain Walsh had left them after they had stripped him down. Dressing quickly, Charlie thought it was appropriate that he would be dressed again when he killed Sonnet. The socks and boots made a world of difference, and while his feet still ached terribly, it was so much easier for him to walk. He breathed a sigh of relief. Sonnet would pay for his aching jaw and his swollen feet. He would pay.

He lumbered along, listening intently, his eyes searching every crevice and every flickering shadow. He sensed he was getting close to the stone arch and paused to listen. Two gunshots snapped loudly in the south; then came three answering shots. So they had moved to the southernmost point of Monument Rocks. He crept ahead. That buckboard was just around the corner.

Cautiously, he craned his neck. There was the buckboard, but it appeared to be empty. When he had passed by a few hours earlier they had been hunkered down in blankets and were sleeping. They couldn't be sleeping now, not with all of that noise. He had been on horseback the last time and had seen straight down into the buckboard. Being on foot put him at a disadvantage. He decided to pull himself into the buckboard to make sure it was empty and then use it as a vantage point from which to level fire against Sonnet when he came along.

Cursing under his breath, he stepped forwards, but then he stopped abruptly. He could smell the woman. A smell like that was something a man never forgot. It was the clean smell of a woman's hair, freshly washed, maybe in a creek.

She must have used some of that pretty-smelling water that he knew soiled doves used when they wanted to get a man's attention.

Charlie stared at the sides of the buckboard. He knew she was in the buckboard; he could hear her breathing. He would kill Sonnet later. Right now he wanted the woman, and he wanted her badly. He clucked his tongue gleefully, and stepped forwards to pull himself up.

He heard a boy's voice say: 'Now!'

Then Jenny Connolly rose up in the buckboard with a Winchester in her hands. In one swift movement she jacked the lever, filling the breech with brass. She pulled the trigger and blew Crazy Charlie's head apart with a .45 caliber slug.

15

Chance Sonnet could sense the coming dawn. There was something tangible in the way the sky slowly transformed itself from a veil of darkness into a world of bright promise and telegraphed its arrival across the barren plains.

He was surprised by the sudden onslaught as the six riders thundered towards the rocks. They spent their ammunition uselessly, firing at shadows. They hooted and yelled for all the world to hear, riding like cowboys on a Saturday night in Dodge City. Their nervousness was evident in their boisterous behavior. They came so swiftly that Sonnet held back from firing for fear of hitting one of the horses.

The riders split up. He watched Charlie canter around as the others made a haphazard pattern in the dust.

Walsh had gone over to the section where the buckboard was stationed near the arch, and Sonnet had remained by himself on the separate cluster of rocks and cliffs. There were few places to climb, but he took advantage of a sloping wall of stone to position himself above any passing rider. He was relying on the darkness to render him invisible, but that would change as the sun began to announce itself in the pale horizon.

From his vantage point he could just make out the stone archway in the distance, but it was still too dark to make out any details. Cabot and his men passed him several times but he held back from firing. They circled wide and some minutes later he heard firing as Jenny and Captain Walsh both opened up from different positions. A man cursed. One of them had taken a hit.

Peering across the plains he saw rifle fire from the archway as a rider passed, but the shot missed. When the rider was out of view he heard another shot. Sonnet hoped that Walsh was keeping Jenny's back covered. Toby would be lucky to hit anything.

The night went quiet. At last a rider came into view, moving in Sonnet's direction. Sonnet was facing the wrong way for a clean shot, but by glancing over his shoulder he tracked the rider's progress. He dared not change position lest any movement attract the man's attention. The rider slowed, moving up behind Sonnet. From his perch on the rock the rider would be out of sight if he moved to his right. Instead, the rider moved left, but Sonnet couldn't swing around fast enough to fire at him.

In that instant he made a snap decision and flung himself off the escarpment just as the rider passed below him. His body slammed into the man, tearing him from his saddle and tumbling them both into the dirt. Sonnet lost his rifle at the moment of impact, and the horse bolted loose. Sonnet felt the wind knocked from his lungs. Black spots danced before his eyes. The other man was on the ground, moaning.

Sonnet pulled himself to his feet. A wave of dizziness washed over him as the other man jumped up, his hand struggling for his gun. Sonnet was too close to draw his own Colt as a rush of nausea tugged at him. He hit the man with his right fist as hard as he could swing it, leaping forwards as the man's head snapped back. His knuckles connected with teeth, knocking them into the man's mouth.

They grappled, and Sonnet took a knee in his groin that doubled him over. Pulling at the man's arm, he yanked the man down with him. He slammed an upper-cut into the man's jaw and heard the chomp as the man bit his own tongue. Dollops of blood burst from his mouth as they fell to the ground.

Sonnet's lungs were on fire. He rasped and sucked air, his chest heaving. The other man was gurgling, his eyes squeezed shut, tears rolling down his cheeks. Sonnet waited as the man regained his senses. After several minutes the man was able to open his eyes; his pain was etched on his face.

'You can ride out,' Sonnet said. 'I don't have anything against you. Just ride out.'

They sat there in the dust looking at each other. Finally the man said, 'I'm Girard Hanson.'

Sonnet nodded. 'I've heard of you. A hired gun. Fast on the draw.'

Girard spat blood into the dirt. He regarded Sonnet through bloodshot eyes, squinting in the gloom as if the darkness had become bright. He stood up, slowly. Sonnet stood up, knowing what was coming, and he was ready.

'I gotta know. Are you as fast as gunslingers like Hank Benteen or Steve Hayes?'

'It doesn't matter,' Sonnet said.

'Why not? Why doesn't it matter? I heard tell you're the fastest gun in the West.'

Sonnet shook his head sadly. 'Go on,' was all he said.

Girard didn't move, but Sonnet saw the gleam in his eyes change, and he felt the tension blowing off the man's body like an evil wind. Girard's gun seemed to jump into his hand, the thumb snapping back the trigger as the weapon swept upwards. Even with that speed, Sonnet moved faster, his gun a blur of motion, the muzzle spewing hot flame. The slug tore a bloody hole through Girard's chest, the lead apparently shattering and deflecting off bone, finally pummeling out of his upper back in a geyser of arterial red.

Girard staggered backwards, his eyes like saucers now, amazed and horrified by his own death, The gun hung uselessly from his forefinger. He dropped to his knees and tried to speak. Then his eyes rolled back in their sockets and he flopped face first into the dust, his legs twitching.

'It doesn't matter how fast those other men are,' Sonnet said to the corpse. 'All that matters is being fast when you have to be.'

Girard's horse had run off, and the night was far too quiet. The gunfire had ceased and there were no other riders in sight. Sonnet holstered his gun and stripped Girard's body of his weapon and its holster. A gunshot sounded off to his right, and as he turned he saw a body tumble near the stone archway. Someone had come too close to Jenny.

Thinking that his own gunshot might have attracted the others, he decided to abandon his perch and find another location. It took him a minute to find the rifle he'd dropped, and with a wary glance at the slowly graying horizon, he hurried away.

There was no reason to stay isolated now, so he made for the buckboard. He was taking a chance because he was vulnerable out in the open. Thinking about Jenny was enough to send him straight towards her. In the distance he could see the crumpled body, but there was no further movement in the buckboard. Jenny had ducked low again.

He was halfway across the open plain when a rider thundered into view, coming around towards the archway. Sonnet threw himself flat, jacked a round into the Winchester and tried to sight down the barrel before the rider could turn the corner. But the rider reined up before crossing the archway, apparently when seeing the body. Cursing, Sonnet launched himself to his feet and ran towards the cliffs. His breath was coming in gulps. He realized then how tired he was. He wasn't just tired from fighting with Girard, but he was tired of all the killing. He thought he had put all of that behind him until Eric Cabot had come to town.

Cabot.

He thought about Lauren, and he thought about his wife and son. Gone too soon. Dust on the wind. Their voices came to him on the night breeze, and then he was up against the cliffs breathing hard.

'Jenny!' he rasped. His back was to the cliff, the rifle at port arms. He heard movement in the buckboard on his right.

'Chance!'

'Are you hurt?'

'No. I shot a man.'

'Good. Is Toby all right?'

'I'm fine,' he heard Toby say.

'This will be over soon. Stay put like we agreed. I'll be back.'

He went left, edging along the rocks. A faint movement flashed in his peripheral vision. A man was crawling out on the plains. That accounted for one of them. Sonnet figured they had abandoned their horses, split up, and were coming at the cliffs from different directions. That would be the smart thing to do, and then try not to shoot each other. Maybe they weren't that dumb after all.

He whipped his head around, scanning the rocks, hoping to spot movement. He needed to pinpoint all of Cabot's men. He knew there were three more, and then Cabot himself. Hunching low, Sonnet held his position, waiting. The man out on the plains was motionless, but Sonnet knew he had his rifle sighted on the rocks. Cursing under his breath, he realized he was in a poor position. If he moved, the man out on the plains would see him and shoot.

Unless something happened to dramatically change the situation, Sonnet was a sitting duck. He couldn't let that happen. He was immobile much longer than he wanted. He went over the gun placement, glanced around to see where he was. The closest gun to him was up near the cliff thirty feet behind him. The rifleman on the plains was angled in the other direction. He would have to empty his rifle and hope for a lucky shot. It wasn't impossible. The range was about 200 yards. But the man was hunkered down in a swell of dirt and brush. He was barely visible in the darkness. Of course, once the sun crested the horizon he'd have a clear shot, but Sonnet couldn't wait that long.

There would never be a good time to fire, but there were plenty of wrong times to start shooting. He was gambling now, and he didn't like gambling. The muzzle flash would reveal his position.

Shoot and run!

He triggered the rifle and the report was like a thunderclap in the eerie darkness. Levering the Winchester, he was on his feet, firing, levering, firing, until the gun clacked empty and he let it fall from his hands. He heard the rifleman yelp in pain as he was running hard. He slipped around a corner just as a rifle barked and the bullet slammed into the cliff three feet to the right of his head. Rock fragments splashed across his face.

So the man was only wounded.

He hit the ground and twisted back to glance out at the plains. The man was gone. But where? He heard the man grunting as he ran. He was stooped low and almost at the point where Sonnet had fired. Sonnet clipped off a shot at the dark figure just as he flung himself to the ground. The shot missed.

The man was too close to the cliffs now and Sonnet would have to reveal too much of himself in order to get a clear shot. A temporary stalemate.

Then something remarkable happened. The man stood up. He grunted in pain as he pulled himself to his feet. His rifle was in his left hand, but his posture indicated he was tired. Sonnet guessed he was losing blood and getting weaker by the moment. The man lurched forwards, coming in Sonnet's direction.

Sonnet kept his finger on his rifle's trigger; a round was already sitting snugly in the breech, the hammer was back. He recognized the man as he stumbled closer. It was Bob, the man who had ridden from camp after the Swede and Sonnet had fought. Sonnet stood up. Bob's shirt was dark with blood, low on his right side. A gut shot. The slow way to die.

Sonnet stepped out and Bob stopped ten feet away. He made no effort to raise his rifle. Blood dripped from his shirt and stained the sandy earth at his feet. His eyes were glazed.

'What happened to the Swede?' was all Bob said.

'A tornado,' Sonnet responded. 'He's gone with the wind.'

Bob appeared to think this over for a moment. 'I'm bleeding bad. I'll never make it back to Dodge in time to see a doctor. It's too far.'

'That it is.'

Bob lifted his Winchester and fumbled with the lever. The muzzle was pointing at the ground but he managed to lever a fresh cartridge into the breech.

'Damn your eyes,' Bob said. He raised his rifle.

Sonnet shot him in the chest. The bullet's impact sent him falling backwards and he landed on the ground with his rifle still clutched in his hands, his mouth foaming with blood. He sputtered and died. Sonnet took the rifle from Bob's twitching hands.

'Shooting you was a waste of good ammunition.'

16

Captain Walsh was hunkered down in a cleft of rocks and watched in amazement as Cabot and his men rode in, making more noise than a soiled dove on Saturday night. They not only expended their energy uselessly, but they wasted a lot of ammunition shooting at shadows. When he heard the sound of gunfire in the section of cliffs furthest from him, he knew that Sonnet had returned fire. His instinct also told him that this wouldn't be a quick and easy battle.

Walsh hadn't been in a gunfight in eight years. A gunfight wasn't something a man sought after, but any man born and raised in Texas knew how to handle himself when the lead started flying. The first thing to remember was to remain calm. He wouldn't fire unless he was sure of his target.

They passed him several times without seeing him, not because he wasn't visible, but because their anger had got the better of them, and they had thrown caution to the wind. Riding hard and shooting at shadows, they had simply not taken the time to slow down and examine their surroundings.

Sonnet had done a good job of placing rifles at various points around the cliffs, but Walsh wished the cliffs offered a better opportunity for climbing. There were few places where a man could climb and remain unseen. The cliffs rose straight up and tapered off, leaving only small ridges and plateaus that were mainly inaccessible. Taking the high ground would have given Cabot's men an advantage. Their goal was to keep them confused, and to keep them moving. Let them tire themselves out.

Dropping to a knee as a solitary rider came into view, Walsh slapped his Winchester to his shoulder and aimed down the barrel. The distance was perhaps too far, but he hoped at least to wound the man. The echo of his shot resounded off the cliffs and he saw the rider jerk. He thought his bullet had clipped him on the left side.

Circling his horse, the man looked around desperately but failed to spot Walsh, who was slumped low in a pool of jagged shadows. Then he spurred his horse just as Walsh fired a second time which, he would soon learn, was a mistake. This time the man saw his muzzle flash. As the rider bolted out of view, Walsh's instinct told him that his position was compromised. He decided to make what he believed would be an unexpected move; he ran in the same direction as the rider, who had disappeared around a corner.

That was his second mistake. As he turned the corner he found himself staring down the barrel of a Colt .45, the hammer back. Eric Cabot's hand looked steady.

'Drop the rifle and unbuckle your belt.'

Walsh did as he was told. The man whom Walsh had shot was standing near by, holding his horse's reins, his hand clutched to his side.

'You shot Lacey, but I reckon he'll live,' Cabot said.

'The bullet just grazed me,' Lacey said. 'Let me show this old coot what it feels like to be shot.'

'Easy now, Lacey.' Cabot studied Walsh. 'Who are you?'

'Captain Sam Walsh, Texas Rangers, retired.'

'What are you doing here?'

'Prospecting. I thought you boys were here to rob me. Why were you shooting at me?'

'That's rich,' Cabot said, raising an eyebrow. 'There's no gold in Kansas, leastways except in banks. But that's good. You're a real storyteller. Where's Sonnet?'

It was good, but Walsh had to admit there was no fooling anyone. 'He's out here somewhere. I expect he has his rifle pointed at your head about now.'

Cabot never flinched. His hand never wavered. Looking down the gun barrel was like looking into the black abyss of eternity.

'He's got a girl and a boy with him. Who are they?'

'I have no idea.'

Cabot hit Walsh on the head with his left hand. The right hand with the gun barely moved. Walsh grunted as the punch struck him under his right eye.

'You had no call to do that,' Walsh hissed.

'Why is Sonnet after me?'

'He'll tell you himself shortly.'

Cabot disengaged the hammer and holstered his gun.

'Tie his hands behind his back.'

'You can't leave him alive. It's like leaving a wounded animal alive. That's always dangerous.'

'Tie him up.'

Lacey cut some rope from the lariat on his saddle and bound Walsh's hands behind his back. The rope bit into his skin.

'I don't like this,' Lacey said. 'Let me kill this old man and be done with it.' He looked about nervously. 'I don't like the way it's got suddenly quiet, and I don't like not knowing what happened to Burnham or Bob or Girard or Crazy Charlie. They should have circled back by now. It's too quiet. There's no wind.'

'You prattle on like an old spinster. That boy and that girl are in the buckboard. We know that much.'

A rider galloped into view — Burnham — and he reined up, eying Walsh.

'Have you seen the others?' Cabot asked.

Burnham shook his head. 'I got shot at a few times, and I saw some muzzle flashes, but I never saw a soul. There's a body by that stone arch, and it looks sort of like Charlie.'

'That's no loss. Help Lacey here get bandaged up. We're OK here for now. We can see anyone coming at us from either direction.'

Burnham helped Lacey clean his wound, dabbing it with a bandanna soaked with water from his canteen.

'Hell, he won't die from that as long as he keeps it clean. What about this old man?'

'I've been thinking about him,' Cabot said. 'He can help us get Sonnet. But we have to get that girl and the boy.'

'They're still sitting in that buckboard with rifles. Can't get near them unless they run out of ammunition or starve to death.'

Cabot's eyes blazed. 'We can't wait that long. We'll take this old man over and palaver with them.'

'She'll start shooting,' Lacey said.

'Then I'll shoot the old man in front of her. Come on. Leave the horses here. They won't wander far.'

They went around the cliffs, pushing Captain Walsh in front of them. When they came around another corner the space before them was open, but surrounded by cliffs on each side. The buckboard was under the arch straight ahead.

'Burnham, you go around the other

way. Lacey, you go along the opposite side. If you two come at her from the opposite side there might be a chance to get that rifle away from her. I'll keep her talking and use the old man as a shield. Shoot the boy if you have to.'

They separated, moving like gray wraiths in the dim light.

In the far distance, a pack of wolves yipped at the increasingly pale horizon.

17

Sonnet was of one mind now: to stop Cabot and his men. Jenny and Toby could hold the buckboard, of that he was certain. But the night had gone eerily quiet and Captain Walsh hadn't made a rendezvous with him as they had discussed.

The sky was slowly growing pale. The stars were fading ever so slowly. There was no movement and no sound. He stood his ground, listening. Nothing. He moved away from the cliffs, crouched low, angling out on to the plains. He wanted to put some distance between himself and the cliffs in order to have a better view. When he was fifty yards out he settled down, lying flat. He took his time and let his eyes take in every detail from that distance.

The cliffs rose skywards like a medieval fortress, the small dark shapes of birds occasionally flitted in and out of small holes or crevices where they had nested. Shadows fell upon the ridges of stone, looking like bloody wounds on a giant's torso. A coyote howled at the sky. The coyote was a long way off, but making its presence known. There was no other sound.

Darkness has texture, and the coming dawn changed that texture, sometimes adding a shade to the palette, which painted the world in a gloomier tone. So it was now. Sonnet was in a dark world and lost in some alien landscape. He was but a shadow himself, an insignificant dash of color in a deadly arena.

When he saw the man come around the corner and make his way stealthily along the cliff face he felt a sudden apprehension. The man moved cautiously, a rifle in his hand. He couldn't make out the man's features, but he knew it wasn't Cabot. He had a memory of Cabot's features from seeing him briefly around town. He would recognize Cabot when he saw him. This man was of medium height, trail-worn, and smart enough to have removed his spurs. So he knew how to hunt a man down without making noise. Sonnet had him figured as a hired gun.

The man stopped, crouched against the rocks. Sonnet watched him set the rifle down and remove his Colt from its holster. He ejected some spent brass and reloaded. He was being careful. When the man slipped his Colt back into his holster and picked up his rifle Sonnet resisted the urge to shoot him. His curiosity had got the better of him. Things were far too quiet. There was no sign of Walsh or the other men. They had come in like raging bulls and then gone silent.

Motionless but for his head turning from side to side, the man seemed intent on something. Then Sonnet realized with a shock that this man was indeed a professional, and somehow he sensed that he was being watched. It wasn't as far-fetched as some might say, for Sonnet himself possessed that instinct for survival that is necessary in all men of action.

The man was looking, waiting, hoping for some sign.

He's good, Sonnet thought, *and I'll bet he's fast. He's got to be real fast with that gun. Maybe he's even as fast as I am. Maybe.*

Girard had thought he was fast. Now his dead eyes watched the sky slowly change color. How many others over the years? They rose before him like specters; vague shapes floating on the air. Cold eyes watched him from beyond the veil. The eyes of dead men who thought they were fast with a gun. All it took to join them was a moment's hesitation, or the reflexes of a man who had practiced for just long enough to be truly skilled in handling a Colt.

Sonnet dismissed his gloomy thoughts. He had to concentrate.

The man was looking at him.

There was no question that this

stranger's keen eyes had picked him out of the shadows. The man slowly turned his body, maintaining his crouched position, and faced himself fully in Sonnet's direction. Time stood still as the two men watched each other. Neither man moved.

Sonnet was surprised when the man stood up, tossed his rifle aside, and then raised his hands. Sonnet stood up and advanced, slowly. He had his rifle in his hands, a cartridge in the breech, the hammer back. His finger rested on the trigger guard. He stopped when he was twenty feet away.

'Did you kill Girard?' the man asked.

Sonnet nodded. 'He didn't give me a choice.'

'Girard was fast. He saved me once from some Apaches down near Tucson. I'm Burnham.'

'I've never heard of you.'

'No, I expect you haven't. I never set out to make a name for myself with a gun, not like Girard did.'

'So why try now?'

Burnham frowned. 'I'm not going to draw on you. I heard you always let the other man draw first, and that you're fast. Since you killed Girard I know I'm not as fast as you. I'm not as fast as Girard.'

'Wise choice. So what now?'

'Cabot's fast, but I don't think he's as fast as Girard. Cabot's after that woman. He's got your friend and he's using him as bait.'

'So you think I should let you go? Will you give your word you won't come after me?'

Burnham nodded, swallowing. He was nervous. 'I need the money Cabot offered. He's got gold and silver in his saddle-bags, and greenbacks, too. Lacey is moving around the other side. Once they get that woman they'll force you into the open. I can help.'

Sonnet didn't like it. Seeing the man ride off would be the better option. Allowing him to keep his guns could be a fatal mistake.

'I have no reason to trust you.'

'I can unload my guns. You can take the cartridges from my belt. All I want is the money in those saddle-bags.'

The man was either a fool or desperate. On the other hand, Sonnet had to make certain he wasn't being played for a fool either. It was a gamble.

'All right. Empty the Colt, and do it slowly.'

Burnham eased his Colt from the holster, holding it gingerly, flipped open the loading gate, and punched out the brass one cartridge at a time. The bullets tinkled to the ground. He holstered his gun.

'Now pick up the rifle and jack those cartridges out. Point the muzzle down to your left.'

Burnham did as he was told: soon the brass bullets were gleaming in a pile next to him. He reached around his holster, pulled the bullets loose from the leather loops and tossed them away.

Burnham said: 'You'll have to be fast to make this work, and there's two of them. Lacey is out there with Cabot.'

'Is Lacey fast?'

Burnham nodded. 'A bit faster than me. I think you can take him, but how are you against two fast guns?'

Sonnet's lips curled into a thin smile. 'I'll manage. Now you get going.'

As Burnham strode away Sonnet thought again about the rifles he had positioned around the cliffs. If Burnham noticed one he would be armed again. Sonnet moved in the other direction, intending to circle the cliffs.

There was no time left for reflection. He had thrown the dice and had to be content to gamble. Following his own tracks, Sonnet glanced at the sky. The darkness was bleeding out and the ghosts would flee from the sun in a very short time.

A gunshot roared from the location where he estimated Jenny and the buckboard were still shadowed by the towering arch. His instincts told him that had been Jenny's Winchester. He hurried now, a nagging sense of dread pulling at his guts.

Coming around the cliff, he faced a wide, open stretch and on the far side there was the buckboard. He could see two shadowy figures closing in. Resisting the urge to shoot, he moved closer.

Then the true nature of Burnham's character was revealed to him. Burnham and Lacey stood twenty feet apart in the gloom facing him. They were the only obstacles between Sonnet and Cabot. Not ten minutes had passed since Sonnet had gambled — and apparently lost — on Burnham. Sonnet looked at Burnham.

'I suppose you loaded your guns?'

Burnham nodded. 'You left plenty of ammunition around, and rifles. This isn't about taking chances, it's about getting something I can rely on.'

'Tell me, Burnham, what can you rely on?' Sonnet's voice was cold. When he spoke, the fingers of both men twitched slightly, eager to get things going.

'I thought about it, and that was right fair of you to give me a chance. Right fair.'

Sonnet thought Burnham was nervous.

'But you can't win here, so I loaded my guns.'

Lacey said: 'What are you, anyway? You think you got Burnham here spooked? You ain't nothin' but a cowtown whore's son.'

Sonnet chuckled. 'I heard about you. Lacey. Burnham said you're fast. Well, I have good news for you.'

'Good news? What does that mean?'

'That means I'm going to kill Burnham here first, and if you aren't running by then I'll shoot you, too, so it's a chance you'll have. I suggest you take it.'

Lacey snorted derisively and he and Burnham pulled their guns.

Sonnet's gun jumped into his hand and the barrel spit fire. His right hand came up and fanned the hammer twice in the blink of an eye as his right hand held the trigger in place. Lacey was fast. He had pulled his gun and had the hammer back when Sonnet's bullet shattered his chest. In his death spasm his finger tightened on the trigger and his gun discharged into the dirt as he toppled over. Burnham's gun had only just cleared the holster when he died.

Sonnet stepped over the bodies and went to find Cabot.

He paced through the gloom with long strides, his eyes piercing the shadows.

He heard Cabot's voice.

'Throw down your gun, ma'am, and you won't get hurt. I represent the law in this territory.'

As Sonnet moved closer he could see that Cabot had a gun to Captain Walsh's head. Sonnet moved closer just as Jenny saw him. She levered a cartridge into the rifle's breech and pointed it towards Cabot.

'She's not putting the rifle down, Cabot,' Sonnet said. 'I want you to turn around slowly so I don't have to shoot you.'

He saw Cabot tense. The urge to spin and shoot wildly must have been tremendous, but Cabot held himself steady. He slowly turned his head to look over his shoulder. Even more slowly, his gun hand dropped away from Captain Walsh's head.

'You have me at an obvious disadvantage,' Cabot said. 'I suppose that shooting I heard means that my men are all dead. I don't even know what this is all about. Why have you been hunting me?'

'There was a girl up north, she hung herself after you left town. Now give your gun to Captain Walsh.'

Walsh took Cabot's gun, and Cabot turned to stare fully at Sonnet.

'This is about a girl?' Cabot was incredulous. 'That girl up in the Dakotas? She was nothing.'

'She was a nice young girl.'

'This is about a girl? Some girl that you knew that died and you're blaming me? You killed all of those men I sent because of a girl?'

Cabot's face was red. His eyes blazed like those of a trapped animal.

'Now I'm going to take it out of your hide.' Sonnet looked at Captain Walsh. 'If his men try to interfere I want you to shoot Cabot first.'

Walsh nodded. He sensed Jenny's eyes on him but he avoided looking at her or Toby. Sonnet cut the rope around Walsh's wrists, handed his rifle to him and unbuckled his gunbelt. Cabot eyed him warily and the two men began circling each other.

'So that's all you want? You think you're man enough to take me with your hands?' Cabot gave a sickly grin.

'Your man Halvar, the big Swede, thought he was man enough, and he almost was.'

Cabot nodded. 'A shame about the Swede. I'll get one or two licks in for him.'

Cabot was on Sonnet in a fury, his right fist slamming into his jaw. He was powerful, but Sonnet had no time to do anything but react. He landed a solid right of his own and followed with a left jab that cut Cabot above his right eye.

He was a bleeder, and soon his face was spattered with his own blood. Cabot bulled into him, and they grappled. Sonnet shot a fist into Cabot's ribs. He heard Cabot grunt in pain, but then Cabot yanked his leg and they tumbled to the ground.

Sonnet rolled and kicked at Cabot's head, but the kick was partly deflected by Cabot's flailing arms. He sprang to his feet in a crouch and as Cabot pulled up Sonnet hammered a fist into his head, his knuckles landing solidly beneath Cabot's left eye. Cabot staggered; his eye swelled up immediately, but it didn't stop him.

Leaping forwards, Cabot landed two hard punches to Sonnet's head, and a third, an uppercut, struck him hard in the ribs. Sonnet felt a white-hot lancet of pain stabbing into his lungs. Cabot growled at Sonnet like a wounded but dangerous animal.

'I hurt you! Now you tell me: was the girl worth it?'

Sonnet spat blood into the dirt. 'Yeah.'

'Then take some more!'

Cabot charged, bent over, and rammed Sonnet in the ribs with his head. Pain exploded behind Sonnet's eyes as another rib cracked and the breath was torn from his lungs. He landed in the dirt nearly unconscious, but with enough sense left to roll and avoid being kicked in the head. Cabot's boot tore into his shoulder. The pain was unbearable, but somehow it brought Sonnet out of his stupor.

He wouldn't remember getting to his feet, but he would remember that gloating look on Eric Cabot's face as he cursed and goaded Sonnet to come on and finish it. Sonnet took a pain-racked breath and laid into Cabot with everything he had.

A right cross knocked teeth loose; a left stunned him. An uppercut took his breath away. A series of hard jabbing hooks disintegrated the left side of Cabot's ribcage. Knuckles busted his nose. Sonnet kicked Cabot in the knee and his boot-heel destroyed that knee.

The blood-lust took over. Sonnet was an unholy thing intent on murder. His fist hammered Cabot's head again and again; he struck him until he dropped to one knee, a line of bright blood dribbling from his shattered nose and mouth. Then Sonnet struck him so hard he thought he might have broken his own hand. Cabot fell face first into the dirt.

'Yeah, it was worth it to see you beaten.'

Sonnet's head ached and black spots swam before his eyes. The only sound was that of Sonnet wheezing and Cabot moaning in pain on the ground. Sonnet was about to turn towards Jenny at last when he heard Cabot uttering incoherent sounds. He was amazed to see Cabot attempting to pull himself up.

'You!' Cabot managed to grunt, one knee off the ground. 'You haven't . . . ' Another wobbly knee came up. ' . . . haven't beaten me!'

Cabot was a monster, bloody and

barely able to stand. 'My father has money. Do you hear me? Money! I'll hunt you to the ends of the earth and watch you die slowly. Do you hear me? You'll die slowly.'

Captain Walsh stepped forwards, and Sonnet noticed that Jenny had come out of the buckboard. She stood next to Captain Walsh, the Winchester still in her hands.

'He's right,' Walsh said calmly. 'You can't let him live. You'll always be looking over your shoulder, waiting for his men to find you again.'

Then, to Sonnet's astonishment, Jenny said, 'That's not the way you and I are going to live together.'

Sonnet saw something in Jenny's eyes that made him pause. Here was something that he had not experienced in a very long time, and it filled him with warmth. He clenched his teeth. All of the madness and grief was still present as well, but now Jenny stood before him like some prairie angel. And he saw something else that made him realize she might be an avenging angel, too.

In the same instant that Captain Walsh raised his Colt, Jenny raised her rifle and they both shot Eric Cabot in the head.

Epilogue

In that hot, silent moment, Chance Sonnet stood with his knuckles dripping blood as the sun burst open the horizon and a ray of sunlight tangled in Jenny's hair. Tears were rolling down her face. Yet, with everything that she had endured, she had not wavered, and she did not avoid his gaze. They all stood there a moment, then Toby came up and said:

'We better clean up your face a bit. You have some cuts from the fight.'

Toby had broken the tension and Jenny helped him clean Sonnet's face and bandage his hands. His wounds were primarily abrasions and cuts from Cabot's punches, and a few cracked ribs that were painful but would heal fast enough.

Captain Walsh occupied his time collecting all of the guns and pulling the bodies together. He set to the grim task of burying them with the shovel from the buckboard, and he buried most of the guns with them.

But he didn't bury Eric Cabot.

He discussed with Sonnet what should be done, and they finally agreed that Walsh himself would take the body to Dodge City. They set out before noon on a hot summer's day, and it was a relief to them when they crossed the Smoky Hill River and eventually returned to the camp where the pine coffin rested in the tall prairie grass.

They made camp again in that place where the Swede had taken to the wind, and Captain Walsh took Cabot's body and set it inside the coffin. Toby and Sonnet helped him slide the coffin into the buckboard. It was late afternoon, the sun was golden, and they drank the coffee that Jenny had made. Jenny commented that it was nice to hear birdsong up in the trees, and even the old oaks appeared to bend in the warm breeze a little as if in agreement.

Sonnet and Walsh talked about the plan again, and it seemed practical enough. Walsh was going to give Sonnet that spread he leased out near Dallas. There was enough land and livestock for him to make a go of it. That night Walsh would take the coffin into Dodge. They drank their coffee and ate some biscuits as the afternoon slipped away, too exhausted to do much of anything else.

Captain Walsh set out for Dodge as the sun was setting. He was conscious of the fact that he was taking a chance. He arrived in Dodge just after midnight. The Longbranch saloon was aglow and the tinny patter of a piano drifted past the batwing doors. Most of the town was dark and only a few oil lamps lit the way. He could hear the steady mooing from the cattle pens and the wind carried the strong scent of cow apples, horses and men too long on the trail. Dodge City was a lot of things to a lot of people, but it wasn't a pleasant-smelling place.

He stopped about midway down Front Street. There was no sign of life. The jail and office of the Dodge City Police Commission was dark. He was surprised. His plan had been to check in and report that he'd found Eric Cabot in the coffin out on the prairie. If the constables had wanted to see where he'd found the coffin he planned on taking them out and away from Sonnet's camp. Any old place out on that windy prairie would do. But now there was no need.

Still not believing his luck, Walsh went to work pulling the coffin out of the buckboard. He pulled it down in the street by tilting it, and then dragging it on to the boardwalk. Cabot was heavy, but it wasn't as difficult as he had imagined. Once he had the coffin on the boardwalk he tilted it up, dragged it into place, and propped it outside the door of the Dodge City Police Commission. He pulled off the lid. Cabot had slumped over on his side, so Walsh took a moment and adjusted him so that he looked a little straighter.

The body was beginning to smell. Looking up and down the street, Walsh was slightly amazed that no one had come out to question him. He knew that if he left now, the result would be the same. Everyone would assume that Chance Sonnet had killed Cabot just as he had said he would. There would be a search of the plains, and a reward would be offered. Walsh, traveling with his ranch hand Frank Neal, Neal's fiancée and her cousin Toby, would say they hadn't seen anyone. They'd keep their eyes open.

Walsh climbed into the buckboard. When he was five minutes out of Dodge City the tension slid away and he felt himself relax. Hell, it was a good plan and it might work. He whipped the horse into a steady trot. He wanted to be as far away from Dodge City as he could get by the time the rooster crowed.

It was still dark when he returned to their camp. Sonnet, Jenny and Toby were awake and waiting for him.

'It's time to move out,' Walsh said. He told them what he'd done and Sonnet nodded. Jenny looked relieved. They began breaking camp and loading their supplies into the buckboard.

When they were ready, Sonnet paused, looking west. It was just before sunrise and Chance Sonnet saw that all of the land was open to them. The day's possibilities were no longer extinguished by a setting sun that burned the sky red. He took Jenny's warm hand in his own and helped her on to the buckboard. Traveling would be easier now that the coffin was gone. The outline of the maples and oak trees swaying in the gentle summer breeze were somehow comforting at last, and while he accepted that on some nights the ghosts that had followed him might still seek an audience, he thought he could manage to live again with Jenny at his side. It was a start, and traveling in the dark wasn't all that difficult. He knew the trail well.

THE GAMBLERS OF WASTELAND

Jim Lawless

Convinced that Blackjack Chancer is behind the death of their youngest brother, Lukus and Kris Rheingold devise a plan. Lukus steals the Saturday-night takings from Chancer's casino, Wasteland Eldorado, and Kris outwits the Marshal and the Wasteland posse as they track him. The Rheingold brothers head for home, followed by the mysterious Lil Lavender, and later by Chancer and his hired gun, Fallon. All three have their reasons for hunting Lukus — and the hunt leads to a final bloody climax in the Rheingold family cemetery.